"Why so angry, Rose? What have I done to deserve this treatment? Could it be something else other than my reticence? Could you desire me to stroke the nape of your neck like this?" His strong fingers gently caressed her nape.

The gesture sent delicious sensations up and down Rose's spine, further weakening her already crumbling defenses. "Please," she whispered.

"Please what?" Richard continued to massage her neck. "Please kiss me? Is that what you want, Rose?" He pulled her closer and brought his head down to hers.

DARING
DECEPTIONS

Patricia Coleman

FAWCETT CREST • NEW YORK

A Fawcett Crest Book
Published by Ballantine Books
Copyright © 1990 by Patricia Coleman

Library of Congress Catalog Card Number: 90-90293

ISBN 0-449-21722-1

Manufactured in the United States of America

First Edition: December 1990

For my family, Sean McKenna, Kathy Morgan, and Jean Ann Caldwell, whose efforts and encouragement made this book possible.

Chapter One

THE MAN KNOWN as Dick August carefully balanced a pint of ale on his forehead while a group of enthusiastically cheering longshoremen made a circle around him. Dick reached for the closest bar wench, grabbed her around the waist, and pulled her into the movements of a stiff-legged waltz.

" 'At's the thing, Dickie. You done it! Pay up, Darby," a longshoreman with salt-and-pepper hair called out.

"Not so fast, Gillis, 'e 'as to make it all the way 'round," another dockworker with grizzled gray hair and heavy weather lines in his face objected. "There, ya see!"

As he spoke, August misstepped and the contents of the precariously set mug spilled down his face and shirtfront, as well as all over his dancing partner. The wench swore at him and jumped back. Dick grabbed her before she got out of reach and planted a loud smack on her lips.

"For you, pretty Meg." He dropped a coin down the front of her blouse.

Meg waggled her hips invitingly. " 'At's more 'n enough fer a dousing, Dickie love. 'Ow do you want your change?"

"Later, Meggie mine, later. Right now I got to

soothe Gillis' nervous condition, I do. How about an arm wrestle, Gillie?"

"Not me, I ain't so daft," the older man refused. " 'Course, if'n anyone else would like to take you on, I'll back you."

No one took him up on the bet. For all his slender frame, Dick August was known to have incredible strength in his arms and shoulders, which he had demonstrated on more than one occasion. The west countryman stood nearly a head taller than anyone else in the room and he exuded a good-humored vitality that made him popular with his fellow ale drinkers.

"I heard that the *Himmelfrau* was anchorin' today." Darby joined Gillis and Dick where they had taken places at a trestle table. "Should be work there in the mornin'. You plannin' on bein' there, Dick?"

"Not me, mate. I got a job unloadin' a nabob's sloop for a golden boy." Dick ran his fingers through his long, uncut black hair and then slid the palm of his hand over his unshaven chin. "Easy money."

"You always seem to get lucky, Dickie boy." Darby shook his head at the wonder of it. "Always got some coins in yer pocket."

"It's Gillie, you see," the younger man turned to his friend. "He's me business manager."

Gillis grinned, exhibiting the solid gold tooth that was his pride and joy. "When you got a chap like Dickie, there's all kinds of possibilities about."

" 'Ere, Darby, come an' settle this," a crony called from another table. "You know all about 'angings. When did 'Ighway John go to the gallows?"

Darby rose and went to settle the dispute, not noticing the slight look of relief that passed between Gillis and Dick August.

"I thought 'e'd never leave," Gillis whispered to his companion. "This come for you, through channels." He slipped an envelope to Dick under the table.

Dick took it and shoved it into his pocket. Casually he stood up and made his way to the alley out back. No one paid any attention to his tall form as he went through the rear door.

Outside, he leaned against the stone wall under the lantern that had been placed there for the convenience of the customers who used the alley to relieve themselves. He pulled out the missive and examined the envelope, finding nothing on the outside. That was as it should be. It must have been forwarded by Sir Michael, who would have taken great care to prevent the exposure of his best agent. Dick broke the seal and removed a sheet of paper, frowning at the heading. It was from his late cousin's solicitor, requesting an interview on Monday next.

That tears it! Dick August, alias Major Richard Augustus Stanton, Viscount St. Croix, thought with disgust.

"It shouldn't be long now, Aunt Bernie," Rose Maynwaring said to her companion. "I can see the spires of Guildford in the distance. They'll fix you up all nice and tight at the Green Man." She pulled her dark head back from the coach window and allowed the isinglass shade to fall into place.

"It must have been the eggs," Lady Dorington replied in a strangled voice. "Normally, I travel very well. It most certainly must be the eggs."

Rose patted her hand reassuringly. "Of course it was. You'll be fine after a good night's rest."

" 'Tis dusk now. I would have thought we'd make better time from Winchester. I must confess, though this coach is very comfortable, I am anxious to reach the Green Man."

"Yes, Mr. Copter certainly did a fine job making the arrangements for our trip. Post all the way to London, the best rooms at the inns, and everything

3

paid for in advance. And we're to stay at Grandfather's London residence, Park House. But, Aunt, why?"

"Obviously, it must have something to do with your grandfather's will." Her aunt raised a lace-edged handkerchief to her lips and closed her eyes.

Rose, seeing this, refrained from further comment. Instead, she lifted the edge of the shade once more and peered out at the bleak February countryside.

Why send for me now? she wondered. Grandfather died six months ago. It must be about the continuance of my allowance. What had the solicitor's letter said? Something about the will having been left unopened until St. Croix's heir could be located. Was that it? Did Grandfather discontinue my allowance? Or perhaps the new viscount sees no reason to continue paying out money for the maintenance of an illegitimate, distant cousin.

She looked over at Lady Dorington, barely visible in the fading light of sunset. The older woman had propped herself in the corner, gripping the handle of her parasol to fight the waves of nausea. How would they manage without Rose's four hundred pounds? True, there was her widowed aunt's pension, but that was not enough to maintain the Tudor manor, Swallows' Walk, that the late Sir Oliver Dorington had left his wife. Rose loved Swallows' Walk from the moment she had come to live with her aunt three years ago. Now, all might be lost.

Rose settled back against the velvet squabs, continuing her thoughts. Perhaps I could become an actress. I was rather good in the plays at the Bath Academy. Does an actress earn enough to keep up an old house and grounds? She imagined herself rivaling the famous Mrs. Siddons. The image of her as Portia, bringing the house to its feet with her stirring "Quality of Mercy" speech played through her mind. The audience demanded an encore, stomping their feet and clapping in an ever-increasing tempo until Rose realized it was the sound of the team's hooves that had speeded up.

"Stand and deliver!" a harsh voice from outside the coach demanded. Its answer was a sharp report from a horse pistol and a sudden lurch as the coach picked up even more speed.

Rose braced herself against the seat to keep from being thrown on her ill aunt. That lady moaned loudly and sank across the cushions.

"We're being waylaid!" Rose exclaimed. Her fingers brushed her reticule. Snatching it up, and then her aunt's, she stuffed them behind the squabs. What else? Rose remembered Lady Dorington's small jewel chest. It was too large to conceal in the seat. Rose grabbed it and frantically thrust it between the carved-roof supports in the hope it wouldn't be noticed. In a last act of defiant desperation, she searched through the food basket until she found a small paring knife. Thus armed, she perched on the edge of the seat, straining her ears to hear what was going on outside the coach. She was tempted to raise the shade but realized it would be foolhardy to expose herself.

The coach careened around a curve in the road, going up on two wheels. Rose slid across the seat. It righted and she slid back. She heard the hoofbeats of more horses galloping alongside. Another gunshot ripped the air.

"Got the outrider!" again the harsh voice yelled even as yet another shot cracked out.

The toe of a boot brushed the window and pushed the isinglass back for the briefest moment. Rose saw the face of their driver as he tumbled past. Bile choked her and she gripped the paring knife tighter.

"After them! No one survives!" the same voice urged on his companions.

The shade flapped wildly with the lurching of the

coach. Rose caught glimpses of two figures, bent low on their horses' backs, galloping to intercept the coach. At the moment she didn't know which she feared more, being in a runaway carriage or the highwaymen who were trying to stop it. She ran her thumb over the handle of the paring knife, desperately searching for some way to change events.

A low moan followed by a faint hiccuping drew her attention back to her aunt. Lady Dorington was struggling valiantly to speak. "Just give them what they want, Rose."

Rose realized her aunt must not have heard the villain's words. The bandits had already committed one murder. They would find it necessary to kill them all.

Two mounted figures saw the driverless coach bolting along the Guildford Road and the four highwaymen racing in hot pursuit.

Richard Stanton pulled out his pistol from its saddle holster and nodded to Gillis. They kicked their horses into a gallop and moved down the ridge on an intercept course with the bandits.

The light was poor and Richard was forced to hold his shot until they were practically on top of the last two robbers. He took out one with his pistol and moved on to the attacker who had managed to climb onto the coach. On his left, he saw Gillis shoot the horse out from under the second bandit, sending the animal and its rider grotesquely somersaulting.

Richard guided his horse to run parallel to the coach. Balancing himself like an acrobat at Astley's, he lunged and caught the top of the coach. With a tremendous heave, he pulled himself up, lying on the roof for a split second to collect himself.

The bandit was busy trying to gain control of the team and bring them to a halt. Richard slid along the roof behind him, hoping to take the man unaware. The highwayman, looking over his shoulder, saw Richard coming and let go of the reins to deal with this new threat.

The two of them struggled, fighting for balance on the dangerously swaying coach top. The highwayman landed an uppercut that sent Richard sprawling against the edge of the roof, his cheek scraped raw by the wood. The bandit, thinking him unconscious, turned back to the team. Richard pushed himself up and attacked the highwayman again, this time getting him in an arm lock. Applying pressure with his powerful biceps, Richard forced the bandit to his knees. Then, in one swift motion, Richard tossed the villain headfirst from the coach. He didn't bother to see if he had killed the man; he didn't care. There were more pressing matters to attend to.

He took up the reins and stood on the brake lever. Gradually the horses slowed and finally came to a halt.

Rose felt the coach lurch to a stop and heard the thumping of boot steps as the rogue climbed down from the box. She braced herself against the side of the door, determined that whoever tried to enter the barouche first would learn he still had a fight on his hands. She glanced down at the puny knife. If only she had a gun!

The coach door was pulled partly open, preventing Rose from seeing who stood behind it. A man's hand snaked in to grab the edge. Without hesitation Rose stabbed at it with the paring knife. The short blade sank into the man's arm just above his wrist.

"What in. . ." Richard's comment ended in a howl of pain. He caught a brief glimpse of dark curls framing the face of an avenging angel before the searing pain obliterated thought. He stumbled back, clutching his arm to stem the flow of blood.

"Last one run off. What 'appened Dickie boy?" Gillis rode up just in time to see his friend's hasty retreat.

"There's a veritable hellcat in there, Gillie." He held his arm up for the older man to see. In a loud voice he continued. "Now I ask you, mate, is this any way to treat a poor longshoreman what's tryin' ta do a good deed?"

At his words Rose peered out of the open door. "Who are you?" she asked, mustering as much authority in her voice as she could.

Had Richard been an ordinary member of the working class, he might have responded to the voice of Quality in the expected manner; by pulling his forelock and asking for the young lady's pardon. But he was not and instead responded with all the brashness characteristic of his chameleon-like personality.

"Why it's just me an' me mate, that's who. The two men what's saved you from a fate worse than death. An' what thanks do we get? A stab in me arm an' demandin' words. Like I'll bleed to death before your very eyes an' all you be thinkin' about is how to move me body out of your way." As he spoke he swaggered back to the carriage and stood arrogantly in front of Rose, raising his wounded arm for her to see.

Rose was taken aback by the man's response. Still, she realized there was a certain amount of justice on his side. "You there," she called to Gillis, "would you get down the small brown valise? I have some bandages and sulfur powder in it." She turned her attention back to the man before her. For a moment she was disconcerted as she looked directly into mocking azure eyes. They peered from beneath dark brows and a shag of ebony hair. His face hadn't seen a razor for days and the stubble was nearly as concealing as a highwayman's half mask. He seemed

8

dangerous in a way entirely different than the frightening experiences she had just gone through. Dismissing the thought as absurd, Rose ducked her head and started to climb from the carriage.

A brown arm, clad to the elbow in a soiled linen sleeve, reached out to help her down. Rose looked up once again into the man's eyes and then darted her own quickly away. Those eyes of his were too penetrating, too discerning. "Could you help my aunt? She's been ill."

"I'll do it, miss." The older man dismounted and looped the reins around the carriage wheel. "Then I'll fetch your bag."

"Thank you." Once out of the carriage, Rose peered back inside at Lady Dorington. "Aunt, we're quite safe. Are you all right?"

There was no response. Anxiously Rose leaned further in and saw that her aunt lay half-conscious.

" 'Ere, lemme take a gander." Richard gently pushed Rose aside and climbed into the coach. He checked Lady Dorington's pulse and was relieved to find it steady. "She'll be all right. Comin' 'round already, she is." He backed out so Rose could see her reviving aunt.

"Leave be, Dick. You'll drip blood all over her ladyship's carriage. Better to let her lie inside, out of the weather." Gillis restrained his friend.

"I'm perfectly capable of picking myself up, young man." Lady Dorington reinforced Gillis's words. "Just give me a hand. I want to see what damage has been done."

Gillis reached in and supported Lady Dorington as she climbed from the coach, her parasol still gripped in her hand.

"Aunt, these are the men who rescued us from the bandits," Rose said by way of introduction.

"We are most grateful. Perhaps you will accept something as reward for your courage? Rose, where

9

is my reticule?" Lady Dorington looked about her.

Richard gritted his teeth. As Dick August it would seem strange for him to turn down a reward, but his personal code wouldn't let him accept one, at least not a monetary one. He eyed the younger woman speculatively. She was a pretty piece, no doubt about it. Courageous, too. Most women of her class would be reduced to hysterics after going through what these two women had experienced.

"T'aint necessary, lady," Richard said, ignoring Gillis's grunt.

"At least let me tend your wounds," Rose spoke up. "Will you ask your friend to light the coach lamps so I can see better?" She took the bag Gillis had retrieved and set it on the ground. It took a moment for her to find the things she needed and to get the small flask of wine from the picnic basket.

"We haven't any water available to clean the wound, but this wine should work just fine. Now, sit here and let me bandage that. I should clean your cheek, too. You've got quite a nasty scratch."

Richard sat down next to a lamp and held out his arm. He watched her face as she bent over her work, taking delight in the way the lamp illuminated the red sparks in her dark hair and glowed softly on her alabaster skin. Her touch was gentle and before he knew it, she had sprinkled sulfur powder on the wound and bandaged it tightly. "It's rather deep. You should have someone stitch it. Do you know a good barber in Guildford? I will gladly pay the expense."

"Gillie'll do it. 'e 'as a fine 'and with a needle. Sewed me up after many a fight."

Rose made no response. Instead, she took up another clean cloth and soaked it with the wine. She gently tilted his head more toward the light and began to sponge off his scraped cheek.

Her soft lips were so near, Richard felt drawn to

taste their gentleness. A gentleman wouldn't do this, he knew, but since when was Dick August ever a gentleman? After all, he deserved some reward. With his good hand he captured the back of her head and pulled her lips down on his. Feather-light though the kiss was, the sweetness of her lips affected him more than the most expensive champagne.

Rose, caught unaware, felt his mouth on hers before she could protest. He pulled her closer, demanding her to respond. Just as quickly as he had begun, he released her.

"How dare you!" Rose sputtered out.

"Young man, that is beyond enough!" Lady Dorington emphasized her words by poking his shoulder with the tip of her parasol.

"Dickie, you've done it now," Gillis remarked calmly.

Richard just grinned.

Rose wanted to wipe the smirk from his face. Rescuer or not, his manners needed minding. In the coldest, most aloof manner she could adopt, she raised an imperious hand to forestall her aunt. "Let it be, Aunt Bernie. We must remember the lower classes are but children who do not know any better. Now, if you will kindly drive the horses on to the Green Man, we should be grateful." She snapped shut the valise and handed it to Gillis. Without a backward glance she walked to the carriage, assisted her aunt in, and followed after.

"Well, I guess you got your comeuppance." Gillis strolled over to his friend.

Richard's grin broadened. "Marvelous, wasn't she? She ought to be striding the boards. I wonder who she is?"

"You're not likely to find out after that bit, mate." Gillie took the lantern and replaced it on the coach. He climbed up to the box and gathered the reins.

"I'll ride alongside, just in case the fourth man went for reinforcements." Richard swung up into the saddle, wincing a bit when he put weight on his injured arm.

The short trip into Guildford was accomplished without further incident. The innkeeper hurried out to greet the coach and sent the stable boys scurrying to see to the horses. After a brief explanation to the landlord, Richard and Gillis disengaged themselves. Richard was about to remount when he saw Rose standing at the entrance.

"I just wanted to thank you again for coming to our aid. It was most courageous of you. I wish you'd accept more tangible proof of our gratitude." She held out a small pouch to him.

"I told you before, lady, t'ain't necessary. An' I hold that kiss more valuable than a bag full o' crowns. With a little practice, you'd be right good at it." With those words, Richard vaulted to his saddle and rode out of the inn yard.

What a cheeky devil! she thought, torn between indignation and bewilderment. She turned back into the inn and made her way to the stairs leading up to the room she shared with her aunt.

As she passed the open door of the common room, she failed to notice the dark figure huddled at the end of the bar. He watched her mount the stairs and silently swore to himself. His employers were not going to be pleased with this night's work. He'd been lucky to get away with his life. The other three hadn't been so fortunate. Ah, well, at least they couldn't be made to identify him now.

"Well, did he take it?" Lady Dorington asked when Rose entered.

"No, you were right."

"Thought so. Strange for a common scallywag to be so gallant. Does my heart good to know that not all the lower classes are cutthroats and thieves. Still, you should have sent it to him by a servant, or at least taken a maid with you."

"That would have seemed a bit high-handed, don't you think?"

"No more than he deserved after his outrageous behavior toward you. What was it you said, something about commoners being children?" Her aunt chuckled appreciatively over the memory.

"Yes, well, it's over and done with. We shan't be seeing either of them again. And I promise to act with the utmost propriety from now on."

"Just be the lady you are. Now, a bite of this delicious meal the inn has provided and to bed. Tomorrow, we arrive in London. I do hope Mr. Copter has notified the servants of Park House of our arrival."

Yes, Rose thought as a small, anticipatory shiver coursed through her, tomorrow we reach London and find out why it was necessary for us to come in the first place.

Chapter Two

Rose Maynwaring stood slightly to one side of the big bay window that overlooked the street and Hyde Park beyond. Her gaze steadily focused on the short bit of drive leading to the doors of Park House. Her fingers tightened upon the golden brocade of the drapes as she saw the black barouche turn off the main road. She dropped her hand to her side, her anxiety marked by the creases in the curtains.

"He has arrived, Aunt Bernie," she said, turning to face the older woman who sat embroidering in a large chair near the fireplace. "However will we pay the money back? Two hundred pounds!"

Lady Dorington placed her stitchery on a small table beside her and looked at her niece. "Rose, it is entirely possible Mr. Copter has sent for you on other business. Perhaps he brings good news. And, if there has been some mistake about your quarterly allowance, I am certain some manner of settlement can be reached. I doubt that Mr. Copter has brought the constabulary with him to throw us into debtor's prison."

Rose crossed over to the seat on the other side of the small table. "You are right, of course, but I doubt that I can hide my nervousness."

"Nonsense. Did you not successfully assume a variety of roles in those little dramas at the Bath Academy? This one will be far simpler, as you merely need to play yourself; the composed, genteel young woman I know you to be." She chuckled at the slight grimace on Rose's face. "Being a lady doesn't mean you have to be a milksop, despite what passes for gentility in society these days. My mother, your grandmother, used to tell us that a lady should be like calm water—still, composed, and, where necessary, applying gentle, steady pressure to accomplish what must be done."

Rose nodded. "I remember, but a lady must also face reality and the reality of this situation is that my paternal grandfather is dead. I, as his illegitimate granddaughter, have no claim on the estate. Yet, for some reason, my quarterly allowance from him has continued for two payments beyond his death. Since I have not been notified that this is in accordance with his will, I can only assume it has continued because of some clerical error."

"Would if be so strange if the old Viscount St. Croix had made provisions for you in his will?"

"More than strange—wonderful. I do not mean to criticize my grandfather unduly, but he never set eyes on me as far as I know. True, he paid for my education and general upkeep, and I am grateful. Still . . ." Rose let her voice trail off.

"Still, he never gave you a home," her aunt finished for her. "I never understood St. Croix. He ignored you, yet he wouldn't let you come live with me in Spain." Her aunt gestured to the chair on the other side of her sewing table. "Sit down and compose yourself." Even as she spoke, she rose and crossed over to the bellpull next to the fireplace. "I'll have Smethwick fetch Mr. Copter after he has brought us some tea. That should be just about the right length of time to establish the impression we wish to make."

When Mr. Copter, of Copter and Lane Solicitors, reached the entrance of the main sitting room, he had a chance to study the two females briefly while Smethwick announced him. One was clearly a dowager in her late fifties or early sixties, but the other was such a delightful incongruity of form, Mr. Copter had to refrain from giving an ungentlemanly exclamation. Rose Maynwaring's face was sweetly youthful, like a barely opened bud, the solicitor thought to himself, waxing metaphoric. Yet her figure was all woman, not one of the needle-thin types that was currently in vogue. Had she been of another class and nature, Mr. Copter thought, she could make a fortune with that unconscious sensuality, rather than live in this state one step above genteel poverty. If she could affect him, a happily married man of forty-six in this manner, the young men of London were certain to flock around her.

"Mr. Fennimore Copter," Smethwick read the name off a calling card, "Solicitor."

"Mr. Copter, how nice to meet you at last." Lady Dorington rose, the younger woman following her example. "Would you care for some tea, or perhaps something stronger?"

"Thank you, Lady Dorington, not at the moment."

"Then please, do be seated." She indicated the settee.

"Actually, my lady, I hope you won't find me too plainspoken, but I would like to get right to the matter at hand."

"Please do, Mr. Copter. It concerns my grandfather's death, I suppose." Rose forced herself to keep her voice steady.

"Yes, Miss Maynwaring, it does. As you know, your paternal grandfather, the Viscount St. Croix, died six months ago." He looked approvingly at the gray half-mourning gown she wore. "In accordance with his last wishes, the terms of his will were kept secret until his heir could be located, a Major Richard Augustus Stanton. Now that has been accomplished and I can inform the principals involved of the terms of the will."

Rose now understood why her quarterly allowance had continued. She felt as if a great weight had been lifted off her shoulders. She wouldn't have to pay back the money after all.

"Miss Maynwaring, you must try to understand that your grandfather never held the circumstances of your birth against you. It was merely the fact that you were female. He wanted an heir of his body to continue the line," Mr. Copter began, wondering how he could discuss the delicate details of the will without embarrassing these two gracious ladies.

"I suppose that is the desire of all men," Rose acknowledged, a defiant edge creeping into her voice. Say what she might, she couldn't quite forgive the late viscount for his treatment of herself and, especially, her mother. "Instead, he got an illegitimate granddaughter."

Mr. Copter caught the edge in Rose's voice, but he was grateful for her forthrightness and understood her justifiable reaction. "Actually, I think he thought more of your mother because she, uh, well, enough on that head. The viscount was obsessed until his dying day with finding a way to continue his bloodline at St. Croix. With that end in mind, he had made a few unusual provisions in his will."

"Do you mean, sir, that my niece's hundred pounds quarterly will continue?" Lady Dorington asked, barely concealing her relief.

"Please, let me explain. The estate of St. Croix is unencumbered and will pass in its entirety to Major Stanton. However, the viscount was an unusual man for his class. He amassed a sizable fortune in addition to the estate. This fortune is not entailed."

"Does this mean Rose will inherit some of this vast fortune?" Lady Dorington couldn't resist asking.

"Yes, my lady."

The dowager couldn't believe the man's obtuseness. "How much, Mr. Copter?"

"A full half, my lady, some five hundred thousand pounds. Provided, of course, she agrees to the viscount's last request."

"Five hundred thousand!" Aunt Bernie fell back against her chair, waving her hand limply back and forth.

Rose was in a state of shock, too. Five hundred thousand pounds! The amount was unreal, incredible. At the moment Rose was quite willing to do anything for the amount. It meant an end to genteel poverty. Aunt Bernadette could spend the Seasons in London, surrounded by her old friends. Rose would be able to indulge herself in her passion for books and music.

"Ladies, please, I must explain the details." He broke into their thoughts. "As I said before, the viscount wanted as much of his direct bloodline as possible to continue at St. Croix. To this end, he made a stipulation in the will. Miss Maynwaring will inherit the sum mentioned, provided she marries the new viscount. If you and the eleventh viscount St. Croix are not married within three months after you first meet, then there is a forfeiture and the total amount will go to Timothy Ralston, a distant cousin in Cornwall."

"Does the new viscount know about these arrangements?"

"I have apprised him of it by letter. I have also taken the liberty of arranging a meeting in my office this Monday for the two of you to meet and discuss the terms."

"And if she

riage?" Lady Do... *ld choose not to enter this mar-*

"Ah, then she wi... *asked.* get nothing, not even

her quarterly allowa...

will the new St. Croix. H...

is the one to refuse, then yo... *pter paused. "Nor*

a settlement of five thousand... *agree and he*

garnered from the interest on... *felt that*

should be settled on you. He felt that s...

would be enough to allow you to live c... *um,*

albeit not in the haut ton."

"Society is not very willing to acknowledge a

out of wedlock, Mr. Copter, no matter what the c.

cumstances," Rose reminded him. She would not put

herself in a position to be ridiculed. She had had

enough of that at the Bath Academy.

"Society, Miss Maynwaring, is extremely quixotic.
In the normal way of things, I would agree and ap-
plaud your good sense. However, in your situation,
things are all together different. The circumstances
of your parents' relationship will, I believe, fire the
imaginations of a society hungry for such romantic
notions. After all, your mother was a beautiful
woman, well liked, and from a good family. She was
engaged to your father at the time of his death. And
it all happened over twenty years ago. Time, Miss
Maynwaring, can turn what was once scandal into a
heroic tale.

"Also, the ton will forgive a great deal if there is
enough money involved. All knew the great wealth
your grandfather had accumulated. It will be assumed that you have inherited a part of it. Of course,
should the fact that you are affianced to the new
viscount be known, your entrée is assured.

"Your grandfather has stipulated that you are to
have complete use of Park House for three months
and enough funds to make your debut. During that

...me you and the new viscount will e an opportunity to become acquainted and e a final decision."
her own and while
Her aunt had a few que awyer, Rose took the
she was putting the ms? really have to lose by
time to think. W ns? At least she and her
accepting th leasures of the city for the
aunt could It was even possible she might
time th roix enough to seriously consider
lik h a rangement. At twenty-one she was
he o reject the situation for mere sensi-
aving a little luck, she might be able to ma-
women. he viscount into being the one to refuse,
weighed the her with a nice income to support the
women. Yes, definitely the advantages out-
weighed the disadvantages.

"February is hardly a good time to launch a debut," Lady Dorington objected. "However, I still
have quite a few friends in London and I think something can be managed. When needs must, etcetera."

"Precisely, Lady Dorington. I hope you have found
everything at Park House to your satisfaction."

"The staff here is excellent. We are quite comfortable, thank you."

"You do understand. This is no marriage of convenience." He didn't seem able to find the right
words to explain the more indelicate aspects of the
will.

Rose realized his distress and smiled. "I understand, Mr. Copter. After all, I am twenty-one and
not some misty-eyed schoolgirl."

"Aunt, can you believe this turn of events?" Rose
exclaimed after the lawyer had been shown out.

"Well, it's about time Athel St. Croix showed a
little grandfatherly feeling toward you. A very
strange man." Lady Dorington paused to reflect for a
moment, then brightened. "But we must attend to

important matters now, girl. I'm sure it h
to you that this quirk of St. Croix's has d
number of possibilities. Three months, th
great length of time, will give you the oppo
meet any number of eligible young men. ____ ____ may
just find someone you can love. I dislike the kind of
arrangement St. Croix demands and will not allow
you to be forced into such a situation," her aunt finished vehemently.

"I must admit, the same thought crossed my mind.
But, I have even a better notion. I shall make the
new viscount be the one to beg off. That way, we will
not have to rely on anyone else but ourselves. With
five thousand a year, we could even repair the roof at
Swallows' Walk and replace the carpet in your sitting room. And don't think I'm being totally unself-
ish. With that income, I could join all the lending
libraries my heart desires and even summer at
Brighton to listen to the outdoor concerts. Truly, I
think that the best plan of action." Rose nodded to
give emphasis to her words.

"That is, perhaps, the most practical approach, I
suppose," her aunt replied hesitantly. "But don't
close yourself to the other possibilities. I would
dearly love to see you happily settled with a man
you could love."

"I'm perfectly willing to fall in love, Aunt Bernie.
I just don't see it as a likely prospect. Most girls
make their debuts when they are seventeen or eigh-
teen; I'm twenty-one and practically on the shelf.
Add to that the circumstances of my birth, and most
would consider me ineligible. Despite what Mr. Copter said, I have had ample proof that my illegitimacy
makes me socially tainted."

"Those uncouth girls at school are not even to be
considered. The solicitor was right about one thing.
Given enough money, society will forgive any past
scandal." Lady Dorington took up her sewing once

n. "I shall arrange for us to meet with Madame
ereaux, the couturiere. Athel can at least provide
us with the necessary clothing."

"Won't Mr. Copter think London's most expensive
dressmaker a bit more than grandfather intended?"

"By the time he gets the bills, it will be too late."
Her aunt tied off a thread and snipped it with a pair
of silver scissors.

While Rose was meeting with the lawyer, Richard
had a rendezvous of his own. Once again dressed in
their longshoreman garb, he and Gillis were entering a modest tavern near Knightsbridge. The common room was crowded with wool merchants,
farmers, and a few laborers. Richard inserted himself between two countrymen and ordered a pint of
ale for Gillis and himself.

"Well, if'n it ain't Dick August. What you been up
to, Dickie me lad?" The jovial bartender filled two
pewter mugs from the huge barrel behind the bar.

"Workin' in the godowns, Johnny." Richard took a
long draft from one of the mugs and handed the other
to Gillis. "I'm supposed to meet me uncle 'ere,
Johnny. You know the one, up from 'Erefordshire.
Seen 'im around?"

"The one what wants you to settle down and scoop
sheep dung?" The bartender chortled at the image.
"He's got the last room at the end of the hall upstairs, as usual. Reserved it, like he always does,
with a letter. Goin' back with him, Dickie?"

"Not me Johnny boy. Me 'eart's not into the
farmin' life." Richard finished his drink and wiped
his lips on the back of his arm. "Well, best get it over
with. Comin' Gillie?"

"I'll stay here an' jaw with Johnny. Yer the man's
darlin'. He'll be waitin' to see you alone."

Nodding at the comment, Richard made his way

out of the common room and up the stairs. At the designated door he rapped lightly and waited.

The door was opened by a middle-aged man in an outdated long coat of brown wool, a functional waistcoat of the same material, and sturdy, thick-soled shoes with brass buckles. He wore a periwig of modest quality tied with a bow of the same nondescript brown.

"Come in, boy. Come in." He held the door wider to allow Richard to enter. Then, after looking down the hall for a moment, he closed it. "Good to see you Stanton." He said, clasping Richard's hand and shaking it. "But it's St. Croix now, isn't it. Congratulations."

"Thank you, Sir Michael, but, at the moment, I feel more like I should be receiving your condolences." Richard began pacing the room even before his superior, Sir Michael Tarasford, could seat himself at the table he was using for a desk.

"Come now, lad, being a peer isn't all that bad."

Richard halted in midstride and turned a baleful eye on the older man. "Our work must be carried on without notoriety. How can I continue as I have now that all of society, and the gazetteers will know my face? I can just see my visage appearing regularly in a Fleet Street cartoon. There goes my anonymity. And the corker is, that inheritance brings a wife."

"So? No one can force you to wed. But even so, why such melancholy? It is a fate we all must suffer," Sir Michael joked.

"Easy enough for you to say, sir. You married Lady Tarasford. If my prospective bride were such a gracious and lovely lady, I'd carry her to the altar, even as you did." The image of a dark-haired angel standing in the soft glow of an inn-yard light rose unbidden for a moment. Or if she had the courage and beauty of a certain young woman, he thought to himself.

"Ah, yes," Sir Michael harrumphed, wishing that particular exploit of his salad days had not circulated among the young men in his command. "But I can see certain possibilities in your situation. Particularly for this next assignment. How is Jacques Dupris feeling these days?"

At Sir Michael's words Richard grinned and subtly adjusted his stance. *"Mais, monsieur, il est très bien."* He accompanied this short speech with Gallic hand gestures.

Sir Michael winced slightly at the heavy Gascony accent Richard used with the character. He well knew that Richard had the ability not only to speak several languages fluently, but to add regional dialects and accents to them that made him fit in to the working class of half a dozen European countries. It was one of the things that made him such a valuable agent.

"Good. But before we get into your next assignment, brief me on the one you just completed."

"There isn't much to tell. Just confirmation of our suspicions. Bonaparte has definitely organized some of the smugglers to try and undermine our economy and bring in his agents. A percentage of the profits is being paid directly into his coffers. I wonder if the haut ton realizes that the money they are paying for smuggled brandy is going to arm troops against England."

"The majority of the landed gentry are far more concerned with their comfort than their country," Sir Michael put in. "But, go on."

"I heard rumors that an envoy was sent to Scotland to enlist the support of the clans. Some of them have ties with France from the days of the Pretender."

"I'll put MacDee on it. But I doubt that the Frenchies will find much help there. Those Highlanders are so suspicious of any outsider that the French envoy will be lucky to even find them. And, with the current administration's more relaxed attitude toward the Scots, most of them are content.

Richard returned to his own report. "The ship movements, according to the German and Dutch sailors and a few of the smugglers, indicate that Bonaparte is relocating his troops. The actual site is difficult to pinpoint at this stage."

"Precisely why I want you to go to Paris. We must know what the little colonel is up to. Also, I want you to coordinate with two Royalist leaders. There are two more contacts that have direct access to information inside Bonaparte's cabinet. It will be a busy trip."

"How soon do I leave?" Richard momentarily forgot his other problems.

"Early next month. There are a few things I need to organize here first. It will give you the chance to try on being the new Viscount St. Croix. In fact, I think it should be the viscount who journeys to Paris. The foppish, slightly dim-witted viscount." Sir Michael made a tent out of his fingers and looked at Richard.

The younger man thought a moment, then shook his head. "The dandy role is too overt, I think. Bonaparte is going to be suspicious of any Englishman. Gambling debts would be better. He is already of the opinion that we English are a dissipated society. For a nobleman to come on the Continent because of embarrassing money problems, that he can comprehend."

"Make him a womanizer, too." His superior suggested. "If anyone can understand problems with females, it's Bonaparte." Sir Michael rose from his chair. "Have you your written report?"

Richard withdrew several sheaves of paper from inside his shirt and handed it to Sir Michael.

"Good. Then I suggest you begin to build St. Croix's reputation. Have you heard of Amelia Wessex?"

Again Richard grinned. "Who hasn't heard of the queen of the Fashionably Impure?"

"I suggest you visit her establishment tonight."

"Right-o, Guvner." Richard slipped back into Dick August's manner of speaking as he prepared to leave.

"You know, some of my colleagues feel these clandestine meetings are melodramatic," Sir Michael said as he escorted Richard to the door. "But I feel it is better to be safe than to make my lads' identities too well-known. Besides, it gives me a chance to show those in my command the old man still has what it takes."

"Not that we ever doubted it, Guv'," Richard said, giving Sir Michael an outrageous wink just before he exited.

Chapter Three

Rose waited in the entry of the Copter and Lane offices in the Temple district while the office boy went to make her presence known to the head clerk. Behind her, one of the maids from Park House stood looking coquettishly at the junior clerks bent over their paper and ink.

Removing her gloves, Rose strolled over to the balustrade that separated the clerks' area from the entrance. Idly she watched the young men working industriously under the supervision of the head clerk on his stool behind a podium. She saw the office boy deferentially approach this dignified individual and indicate where she waited. The middle-aged man descended from his exalted position and made his way over to Rose.

"Miss Maynwaring, I'm Mr. Stykes, the head clerk. Mr. Copter is expecting you. If you will follow me please. Your girl can wait for you over there." He indicated a wooden bench against one wall.

To hide her nervousness, Rose thrust her hands deeper into the silver fox muff she carried and secretly twisted her gloves within its concealing depths. Her plan just had to work. Certainly any man, especially a military one, would think twice before marrying a—a love child. Her thoughts stumbled over the appellation. All she need do is make certain Mr. Copter tell the new viscount her background. Once he begged off, she would retire from his presence in wounded dignity. That was it—noble to the end. Here she started to chuckle but quickly changed it to a cough when Mr. Stykes turned a questioning eye on her.

"Them be the junior partners, miss." Mr. Stykes gestured to two sets of doors facing each other at the top of the landing. A short hall branched right and left, ending with two massively carved oaken portals. He led her to the one on the right, knocked, opened the door, and announced her arrival to the room's occupants.

Richard paid no attention when the head clerk announced the arrival of Miss Maynwaring. His back was to the door as he looked broodingly into the embers of the hearth. He had already made it clear to Copter that he would have no part of this fiasco. He was not, he had told the lawyer, the sort of man who would allow another's will to dictate to him. The lawyer had picked up on the pun immediately and they had both had a good laugh. Now, all that remained was breaking the news to the woman. That would be more difficult. From what little Copter had told him, she had been living barely one step ahead of the bill collectors. Perhaps he could do something about that. After all, she was a relation, albeit a distant one. Strange that old St. Croix hadn't done more for the chit. With these munificent thoughts, he turned around and immediately abandoned his altruistic plans.

How rude, Rose thought as she stared at the back of the tall man by the fire. Just because the pose lent a decidedly romantic air to his lean body and broad shoulders was no reason to stand with his back to a lady. He must be one of the junior partners Mr. Stykes mentioned, Rose decided, and looked around to see if anyone else was in the room. There being no one to fit the image of St. Croix she had created in her mind, she concluded he hadn't arrived yet.

"When shall the viscount be joining us?" she asked innocently.

It was at that moment Richard turned and beheld the face that had been lingering in his mind's eye. She seemed different, yet he would know those flashing eyes and soft lips even if she were wearing a loo mask. Gad, what curious fortune has been dealt me this time? he thought, even as he reached out to brush his lips against her hand. On impulse he turned it over, palm up, and gently kissed the sensitive spot inside her wrist. "I'm St. Croix."

Rose was too startled to do more than form a little "oh" with her lips. Belatedly she remembered her manners and bobbed a little curtsy. She felt totally thrown off balance. He was at least six-foot-two, and rather than the slightly aging figure of her imaginings, his figure was whipcord tight, with broad shoulders narrowing to a small waist and down to well-formed thighs displayed in kerseymere breeches. She snapped her eyes up and found herself staring into amused, azure orbs. The humor she saw there stiffened her backbone. He was laughing at her!

Richard assessed her coolly, though he couldn't help but be amused by the look of confused surprise that had flicked across her face when she first learned his identity. For the briefest of moments he wondered if she would recognize him as the vagabond who had rescued her from the highwaymen and stolen a kiss. When he saw no sign of recognition, he relaxed. Already he was beginning to plan how he could balance his latest assignment with this pleasant development in his personal life.

"Perhaps we should discuss the matter at hand," Mr. Copter interjected, sensing the time was right to resolve all the details. "Miss Maynwaring, would you care to be seated?"

Rose lowered herself into the chair opposite the solicitor's desk and folded her hands demurely in her lap. Out of the corner of her eye she saw St. Croix take the other seat.

"I think we can dispense with beating around the bush," St. Croix said flatly. "With Miss Maynwaring's permission, I shall enter the announcement into the papers today."

Rose stiffened. That was it? He sounded more like he was contracting for a horse at Tattersall's. Obviously he must need the money very badly. She'd have to do something quickly to turn the situation about.

"That would be acceptable," Rose assured him, keeping her own voice level. "If you could have your secretary prepare a list of those you wish to invite to the ceremony, I shall see they receive an invitation."

Mr. Copter felt like something had slipped past him. Here were these two very attractive people treating each other like they were made of ice. "I believe, before the announcement or the invitations can be ordered, a date must be set."

"Of course," the viscount said. "This is February tenth; the second Sunday in March would suit my schedule. Is that acceptable, Miss Maynwaring?"

"Quite acceptable, my lord."

"Then I'll bespeak St. George's for that day. Is there anything else, Mr. Copter?"

Both pairs of eyes turned expectantly toward the solicitor.

"Well, ah, no," he replied, feeling somewhat breathless from the proceedings.

"Fine, then. Miss Maynwaring, permit me to drive you back to your home." St. Croix rose from his chair and offered his hand to her.

Rose hesitated. She had been outmaneuvered, but

there was still time to turn things around. How to bring the subject up?

"Surely, you aren't afraid to be alone with me in a carriage?" The viscount's voice held a note of challenge. "After all, we've just become affianced."

"Certainly not, my lord." Rose snapped, then modulated her tone to one of cold politeness. "I thank you for the offer and gladly accept."

She doesn't sound too glad, Richard thought. He took it as a good sign. At least there was more substance to Rose Maynwaring than a pretty face and voluptuous figure.

"Just a moment, my lord," Mr. Copter said before the younger man could go further. "There are a few details that must be settled first."

"We can discuss the business end of this affair at another time, Mr. Copter. I would not want to bore my betrothed with such unfeminine details."

Rose turned measuring eyes on the viscount. Here was her chance. No man would want to marry an anxious and managing woman. Add the circumstances of her birth and he must beg off.

"I believe Mr. Copter is right, my lord. The sooner we clear away such matters as quick rents and percentages, the more at ease we shall be in each other's company. Speaking plainly, we are both agreeing to this situation because it is of tremendous financial benefit to us. Something else, Mr. Copter," Rose said, turning back to the solicitor, "I want the viscount to know all about my background."

Richard reseated himself and leaned forward at that.

"Tell me, Miss Maynwaring, do you have the Venus disease?" he asked, looking directly into her sienna eyes. "For, I fear that is the only thing that might cause me to waver from my chosen course. Mind you, I said waver, not deviate. That would depend on just how badly you have it."

31

Much of what he said was lost to Rose after his first direct question. Her eyes widened in shock and surprise. "No, of course I don't have, have that. I've never even been in a situation where I might, I mean . . ." Rose became flustered.

"Well, then, nothing else is of any importance. I can assure you that I am not so afflicted, either. Therefore, we needn't worry about our progeny." St. Croix feigned relief.

Mr. Copter was beginning to feel more like a nanny dealing with precocious children than a respected member of the bar negotiating with two members of the gentry. "My lord, there really is no need," he began.

"Quite right, Mr. Copter, there is no need. My man of business will get in touch with Miss Maynwaring's man of business if there are any problems to be worked out. All you need to see to is the final marriage agreement. I am fully aware that Miss Maynwaring will receive one half of the unentailed properties. I have no argument with that. So what is left to discuss but the more pleasant details?"

St. Croix was already out of his chair and standing behind Rose. The solicitor could do nothing else but rise himself.

"Miss Maynwaring, my phaeton is at your disposal," the young viscount said.

"Ah, thank you, my lord." Rose gathered up her gloves and prepared to leave. "Thank you for your kindness, Mr. Copter. I hope I shall be seeing you again, soon."

"My pleasure, I do assure you, Miss Maynwaring." The solicitor escorted them down the stairs to the street entrance.

Rose took in a deep breath once she was outside. Glancing at the clock on the building opposite, she realized with a start she had been in the office for less than thirty minutes. In half an hour her entire future had been changed. She cast a surreptitious glance from under her toque hat at her escort. He is a handsome devil, she thought, and a cunning one. Why would someone like him want to agree to this absurd marriage? Could he be so strapped financially that his motives are the same as my own? If so, I'm hardly in a position to condemn his actions.

"Miss Maynwaring, if you please," his voice intruded on her thoughts.

She crossed over to where he was waiting to assist her into the phaeton, having waved away his tiger. She placed her hand in his, thinking how small it seemed by comparison. A flash of nervousness coursed through her veins. "My maid," she began.

"I've given her a guinea to take a hackney home. There isn't room in the phaeton." He handed her up to the seat.

Rose looked down at him, about to protest. His face was at a slight angle and his eyes gleamed with challenging mischief. For the briefest moment she felt as if she knew him from somewhere else. Before she could examine the thought, it was gone and Stanton was climbing up beside her.

"Aboard, Jakes?" he called back to his tiger.

"Right-oh, my lord."

With that Richard urged the horses forward.

"I thought a cup of tea might be in order. There's a very pleasant little kiosk in Hyde Park where we can relax. We two have a great deal to discuss," Richard said easily.

"Indeed we do, my lord. But I'm not certain a public tearoom is the place for the discussion. I am a single woman and I have my reputation to think of," Rose protested mildly, a glint of humor warming her eyes.

"Your reputation will not suffer a jot if you are

33

seen having a refreshment with your affianced. But I can see you aren't the least serious, so it's to the park."

Despite Richard's attempts to engage Rose in a discussion of their situation during the rest of their drive, she would guide the conversation into other channels. When she turned the talk into a debate on Napoleon Bonaparte and the recent Treaty of Amiens, Richard gave up. Obviously the lady had no intention of opening up about herself.

"What is your opinion, Miss Maynwaring? Can we British trust Bonaparte?" he asked, conceding to her wishes temporarily.

"I suppose," Rose began, "that the man has been of tremendous benefit to his country. But, I cannot feel that we should trust him. France has always wanted to dominate England and this little colonel is a personification of that ambition."

"There are many in England who would agree with you," Richard said as he pulled the phaeton to a stop before a charming wooden structure shaped like a Chinese pagoda.

Jakes ran to hold the horses' heads. Richard climbed down and circled behind the carriage to come up on Rose's side. She let him help her, feeling a bit breathless when he placed his hands around her waist and lifted her without seeming effort.

Inside, the proprietor had a warm blaze going to ward off the February chill. Richard escorted Rose to a small table by a window overlooking the park. He placed the order, then turned his attention to the woman opposite him. She was studying the view and the soft winter light lent a dream-like quality to her features.

"And now, Rose, where should we begin?"

"I don't recall giving you permission to use my given name," Rose countered.

"Very true, but we are here, unchaperoned, and that does imply a certain intimacy between us."

Rose gave a rueful smile. "Another strategic move, my lord? Very well, Richard and Rose it shall be, though it sounds like something from a primer. You know, 'Richard and Rose raced rapidly round the rooster.' "

"I remember those. I believe I had one about Plain Peter, or some such character. But, tell me, are you always so docile? Rose, where are your thorns?" Richard mocked lightly.

"There is no point in wasting ammunition in minor skirmishes that can be used in more important battles, is there, my lord?"

Richard read the challenge in her eyes but refused to rise to the bait. Instead, he responded with, "Well, we need to marshal our forces if we are going to convince society at large we are the happy, devoted couple."

Rose stiffened her spine at his words. What ploy was he engaging now? Surely he had no intention of their relationship being any more than the common definition of a successful society marriage. Slowly, as if she didn't care what he answered, she asked, "What does it matter?"

Richard reached across the table and took her hand. "It matters to me. You shall be my wife and I will not have you, or myself for that matter, subjected to innuendo and gossip. True, it is common practice to marry for reasons other than romantic ones, but I loathe the wagging tongues and coy glances when such distant couples enter a room. I will not have it for me and mine."

The words *me and mine* echoed inside of her head. They sounded so possessive, so primeval. If only there was love behind them. It would be very easy to fall in love with this man, Rose thought. His compelling good looks and powerful physique emanated an almost magnetic pull on female heartstrings. There was an air of mystery, no, more like danger about him. The kind of danger mothers warn their daughters about. What does a man like this want with the sort of marriage her grandfather's will demanded? It had to be the money. Is that what he meant by "me and mine"—his money? "And just what can I expect from our relationship, my lord?"

Richard realized he had stepped dangerously out of character and pulled back into the persona he was establishing for his new assignment. Rose must not suspect that he was anything more than a jaded member of the ton. For her to know otherwise could be dangerous for them both. "What any other society marriage is, I expect. I shall make very few demands on you beyond being a gracious hostess when I need one. I, in return, shall escort you to those balls and fetes you deem important."

That hardly sounded like the kind of relationship her grandfather had had in mind, Rose thought. Hadn't Mr. Copter explained the full terms of the will to the new viscount? How could she, a woman, broach such delicate matters with a man she had just met? But Richard was continuing on and Rose forced her attention back to his words.

"As for the remaining terms of the will, once we are married that will be an end of it."

"Isn't that a bit underhanded?" Rose's basic honesty forced her to ask. Despite her embarrassment, she pushed on. "After all, from grandfather's point of view, there is only one reason for all this elaborate legal manipulation. That was to produce an heir of his bloodline."

Richard hadn't let go of her hand and now he tightened his grip on her fingers. "I don't mean to imply that we will have no children. But it shall be when we, with the help of God, wish it."

He was saved from having to say any more by the arrival of the tea and cakes. As she poured the amber liquid into the cups, he directed the conversation back to their earlier discussion of France.

Rose followed his lead gladly, too shamed by her earlier boldness to speak. Instead, she pondered what he had said. It was perfectly clear that St. Croix had no intention of declining the marriage now. She was caught. But what an enigma he was. Had she really detected concern in his words? Or was she trying to find something that wasn't in the man? Some foolish dream from fairy tales and schoolroom fantasies? Her thoughts were interrupted by his question.

"I said, I hope you will like Paris."

"Paris?" Rose repeated the last word he had said.

"Yes, Paris. For our wedding trip."

"Oh, I hadn't thought about, I mean . . ."

Richard let her stutter on, finding her confusion charming. "What you mean to say is that you hadn't expected, when you entered Mr. Copter's office today, to leave it an engaged woman. I was perfectly aware of your manipulations, my dear. A more fainthearted fellow would have succumbed immediately. However, I am not so lily-livered, and I give you fair warning, no more of your, ah, strategies between us. I have no doubt you learned your tactics on the chessboard. But I, my dear, learned mine on the battlefield. There is little doubt which of us would be the victor should you try to pit yourself against me." Then, seeing the look of amazement on her face, he went on in gentler tones. "Let us pool our resources. As for Paris, with the new treaty it is once again safe for the English to go and enjoy the sights of the Continent." He looked into Rose's carefully schooled face and wondered what was going on behind that oh-so-proper expression.

Paris, she thought. Why Paris? True, it was a city

like no other in the world, but why now? The political situation, despite the treaty, was still too uncertain to make traveling safe. Could it be that St. Croix longed for the dissipations the city was famous for? "Paris is a city I have long desired to see," she said crisply. "As for your earlier words, my lord, they sounded very much like a challenge."

"And do you intend on picking up the gauntlet?" he couldn't resist asking.

"To answer that would be a tactical error," she replied lightly.

Richard acknowledged the remark with a grin and turned the conversation back to more neutral topics. By the time they had finished their tea and made the short trip back to Park House, they had slipped into a companionable rapport. He helped her down before the brick town house, but shook his head when she asked him in.

"Not this time, I'm afraid. I've an appointment I must keep."

Rose watched as he climbed back up the high-driver's seat and took up the reins. He gave her one more jaunty wave, then snapped the leathers to start the horses moving. When he made the turn at the end of the street, Rose recollected where she was and hurried up the three steps that led into the house.

Her aunt was waiting for her in the drawing room. "Well, pet, tell me what happened."

Rose plopped herself down on the petit-point sofa and regarded her aunt for a moment.

"It seems I am to be married," she finally replied and began to recount the incredible events of the afternoon.

Chapter Four

LADY DORINGTON RAISED the silver teapot and poured more of the amber liquid for the lady sitting across from her.

Their guest accepted the cup. "I must tell you how pleased Lord Beresford and I are that you are allowing your niece to make her debut at our ball. Society is so thin this early in the Season, and, for her sake, I wish it were otherwise."

Rose put down her own cup and smiled at Lady Sarah Beresford. "That is most kind of you to say. But it is I who must thank you for your assistance in this matter of entering society. It is truly very kind of you to help a stranger."

Lady Beresford gave a little dismissing wave to Rose's words. "Stranger? Not at all. Bernie and I have been friends since the schoolroom. It is my pleasure to present her niece. I knew your mother, too. Sweet, beautiful woman. So sensitive to others."

Rose found herself looking for signs of censure in Lady Beresford's words, but the older woman was quite sincere. Would she always tense at the slightest referral to her past? It was foolish to be so thin-skinned. Yet, it was a bit like waiting for the other shoe to drop. Sooner or later someone would connect her with the old scandal.

"Rose, Sarah was saying that she plans to do the ballroom in shades of cherry pink and white. Won't that be lovely?" Lady Dorington called her niece's thoughts back to the present.

"I wanted you to know so you could plan your gown accordingly. It would be simply awful if you clashed with the setting. We have hopes that the Beau will attend. He's in town at the moment."

"Beau Brummell is in town? I thought he was in Tunbridge Wells doing the pretty with the prince." Aunt Bernie helped herself to one of the tea cakes.

Lady Beresford nodded. "He was, but now he's back. Prinny is continuing on to Bath, or so I hear. But you know the Beau's ways, he can't stay away from the tables long."

"Gambling will be his undoing." Aunt Bernie commented. "Tell us, Sarah, any other *on-dits* circulating around town? We would not like to appear as country bumpkins at your gala."

"Well," Lady Beresford warmed to her subject. "There is the new Viscount St. Croix. Handsome as the devil himself, and so tall!"

At the mention of Richard's name, Rose took more interest in the conversation.

"They say," their guest continued, "that he's been frequenting Amelia Wessex's establishment and losing every night at her tables." She paused, completely ignoring the frown on her old friend's face. "It is also common knowledge that he seeks comfort from her, ah, employees. Some say Amelia herself welcomes him into her boudoir. Oh, dear, I do get carried away!" Lady Beresford belatedly remembered the presence of an unmarried girl in the room.

"Sarah, please, I think you should know that we have it on good authority that those rumors are quite false." Lady Dorington glanced worriedly over at Rose. Her niece seemed completely composed, but the older woman wasn't fooled. "I suppose it will not hurt to tell you, though I must have your promise you will not spread it about until the announcement appears in the *Gazette*. Sarah, Rose is engaged to marry St. Croix. I am certain the gossip you have heard is no more than that. You know how it is. A young handsome peer comes to town and everyone is ready to attach all sorts of stories to him."

Lady Beresford was sincerely regretful over her ill-chosen words. "My dear, you mustn't pay any attention to what I said. Tales have a way of growing all out of proportion."

"Quite right." Aunt Bernie nodded agreement. "Why, I suspect poor St. Croix went to this Wessex woman's establishment with a group of friends once, and on such scanty evidence, this story was built. Think no more of it, Rose."

But, how can I not think of it? Rose wondered. St. Croix has been in town scarcely longer than I have, and his name is already being bandied about. It could be as Aunt says. The vague, all-encompassing *they* Lady Beresford referred to usually didn't exist except in the ill-chosen words of tittle-tattles. But, it did give her cause to wonder.

"Will St. Croix be escorting you to the ball, then? I am so looking forward to meeting him. I shall extend an invitation right away." Lady Beresford gave Rose a little, conspiratorial smile. "Tell me, Miss Maynwaring, is he as tall and as handsome as they say?"

"Indeed he is. Quite a giant of a west countryman." Rose returned her smile.

"West countryman? Heavens, don't tell me he is one of those rustic creatures?" Their guest was genuinely surprised to hear of St. Croix's origins.

Rose's smile widened. "He's from Cornwall, actually. He has the dark hair and blue eyes one sometimes finds in the region. But do not fear, Lady Beresford, he is quite domesticated."

The older woman flushed a bit, embarrassed by her rude comment. "Of course he is. Please forgive my words. I meant no slur to the viscount. Actually, I have heard that men from that part of the country have a certain *je ne sais quoi* about them that attract women as a magnet does iron."

"Like in a Radcliffe novel, I suppose," Rose offered.

"Yes, precisely." Lady Beresford nodded agreement and then saw the glint of humor in her companions' eyes. "Now, really, Miss Maynwaring, that was too bad of you. You have made me confess that I have read novels that no woman of my age is supposed to have any interest in." She began to gather up her reticule. "I really must be going. This has been a most delightful morning call. It is so good to talk with an old friend." She hugged Lady Dorington and extended her hand to Rose.

"We were delighted you could come." Lady Dorington walked with her friend to the door.

When her aunt rejoined her, she looked with concern at Rose. "That Sarah Beresford could talk the ear off an elephant. You mustn't take anything she says to heart, gel. In school we called her slip-tongue Sarah because she prattled on so."

"Then you think there is nothing to these rumors about St. Croix?" Rose asked.

"I think that St. Croix has probably behaved just as any other young man come to town. But, if you are having second thoughts, you need only say so and we will be off to Swallows' Walk this afternoon."

Rose shook her head. "I can't do that, Aunt Bernie. I gave my word and I am honor bound to keep it. Besides, it must be as you say. I am certain there are just as many rumors flying around about me and the circumstances of my birth as there are about the viscount." And my appearance at Lady Beresford's ball will bring them all back into society's mind.

Will Lady Beresford's *they* accept me, knowing all this? Will I have to suffer walking into the ballroom and seeing the scorn and derision in a hundred pairs of eyes?

"What are you thinking, gel? You seemed quite in another world." Her aunt's voice broke into her thoughts. "We have much to attend to today. Madame Vereaux has already arrived and awaits us in your chamber for the final fittings of our gowns. Then we must pay a visit to Bond Street and make a few purchases. I should like to stop at Gunther's after that. One of their raspberry ices would prove most refreshing after the shopping."

Rose gave a little laugh. "My goodness, Aunt, you have it all organized as any general planning his campaign."

"Indeed, Rose. A debut is far more complex," her aunt replied in a bantering tone. "Now, madame awaits."

"All right Gillie, earn your pay as a gentleman's gentleman," Richard handed the older man his neck cloth and bent his knees to make it easier for Gillis to tie it properly. "Make it a Mathematical. St. Croix is nothing if not fashionable."

"You're in a sprightly mood, Major. Stepping out with your lady?" Gillis folded and tied the cravat in the intricate pattern Richard had requested.

"That I am, Gillie. Tonight's our first official appearance as a betrothed couple. The Beresford gala. Pity it's so early in the Season. Miss Maynwaring deserves to have more entertainment than the few routs and balls that February has to offer." He straightened when Gillis finished tying the neck cloth and took up a waistcoat of embroidered yellow velvet and looked at it distastefully. "Bit strong, don't you think, Gillie?"

"You are supposed to be a tulip, Major. Yellow is a

43

very fashionable color at the moment. It won't be so bad with the black breeches and coat."

"I suppose you're right. This St. Croix fellow is the hardest role I've ever adopted. But we must remember St. Croix is a gambler and a philanderer, not a fop." He grimaced again and put on the vest. "I don't like being a social darling, Gillie. I'm not cut out for it."

"Be that as it may, Major, it's the St. Croix Sir Michael wants."

"Ah, yes, duty above all." Richard said these words strongly, for they were his code. "And speaking of duty, I'm not the only one to play a role tonight. I want you to go to that club that all the valets frequent, what is it, the Bow and Fiddle?" Seeing Gillis's nod, he continued. "You, as Hamstead, my not-so-content manservant, are to confide in your fellow valets the arduous task of being in my employ. You may hint that I enter into this marriage for financial reasons and strongly suggest that I will bring about the ruin of the St. Croix fortune if I do not mend my evil ways."

"Aye, sir. I'll single out the biggest gossip in the place. A word here, a hint there, but not too much. We upper servants are supposed to be discreet." Gillis grinned, flashing his gold tooth. "But you be careful tonight, Major. They say the waters of society are more treacherous than the Caribbean."

"Why, Hamstead," Richard drawled in the effected speech fashionable at the moment, "you wax metaphoric on me." He took up his evening cape and gloves and waited while Gillis opened the door. "Enjoy yourself, Hamstead. I shan't be needing you until late."

Rose entered the main salon of the Beresford house flanked by Richard and Lady Dorington. They had arrived fashionably late, and the dancing had already started. She watched as the ladies in the brilliant jewels and gowns swirled around the dance floor in a waltz, held by gentlemen in equally splendid evening dress.

"Rose, remember, no waltzing until you have been given permission. St. Croix, I depend on you to keep Rose from unwittingly committing some faux pas. Everyone will be curious about you and you will be under the closest scrutiny," Lady Dorington warned them. "I shall take my place, over there by Lady Jersey and Mrs. Paxton. They are always filled with the latest gossip."

Rose and Richard escorted her to the other ladies and introductions were made. The formalities over, Richard asked Rose to join him in the quadrille that was forming.

"I should like that, my lord. But I warn you, I have little experience dancing."

"What? Is there no dancing at Swallows' Walk? I had no idea you came from such Cromwellian surroundings."

"Nonsense. There were local parties, of course, and an occasional assembly in Winchester, but I fear my experience is limited."

Richard smiled to reassure her. "Fear not. The quadrille is such a lively dance, no one will notice if you misstep."

They began the movements, each couple moving to the center of the square they formed, passing under the arms of their partners, and stepping to the two-four time of the music. When the set was over, Rose was glowing with the exercise.

"Would you fetch me some punch, Richard? The dancing has left me very thirsty."

"Of course. Just let me escort you back to your aunt. I see she is in deep conversation with Lady Jersey, arranging for your vouchers to Almack's no doubt. But be wary. Lady Jersey is a notorious gossip monger, though there is no real harm in her."

Rose looked up into his blue eyes. "I had no idea you were so familiar with the patronesses of Almack's. What other surprises do you hide, my lord?"

"Ah, Rose, I stand before you a perfectly mundane man, full of human frailties. And here you are, safely returned to your protecting dragon." He spoke low, leaning close to Rose so Lady Dorington did not overhear the remark.

While Rose and Richard danced, Lady Dorington had been listening to the newest *on-dits* from her two companions. The fact that Richard figured prominently into many of them did not please her in the least, though she hid her concern.

"But isn't your niece engaged to St. Croix?" Mrs. Paxton asked. She had a malicious streak in her and had been the main conveyer of the gossip.

"To be sure, she is." Lady Dorington was not about to add any new information to the tittle-tattle's supply.

"It is not unknown for even the most hardened rakehell to reform upon meeting the right woman," Lady Jersey tried to soften Mrs. Paxton's implication. "And Miss Maynwaring is such a lovely and gracious girl, I'm certain such is the case here. After all, St. Croix hasn't done anything *really* inopportune."

"They say," Mrs. Paxton refused to let go of the topic, "that he dropped three thousand pounds at the gaming tables in less than three hours and didn't even blink. Is he really so wealthy he can afford such losses, Lady Dorington?"

"The viscount's financial matters are no concern of mine." Lady Dorington refused to be drawn in.

"He must be as rich as Croesus. Why, I heard that he bought that Wessex woman a yellow carriage and four matching white horses just so she can drive in the park during the fashionable hour. Some say he even paid for her box at the theater. Oh, dear, Bernie darling, I do not mean to cause you distress." Lady Jersey waved her fan before her face and regarded Lady Dorington over its edge.

"Have you seen this carriage?" Lady Dorington turned toward her. "Rumors, no more. All young men have their interests. St. Croix is no better or worse than the others, Sally."

"Quite right. And he does seem taken with his fiancée." Lady Jersey indicated where Richard and Rose were approaching them.

Richard did not miss the hard look Lady Dorington gave him and, knowing her two companions, he could judge why she was out of sorts with him. The things I do for my country, he thought sardonically as he went to fetch the punch cups.

When he returned, he was disgruntled to see Rose surrounded by young men, many he knew to be rogues of the first order. One, Stykes with his ever-present companion Trumble, was even under suspicion of acting in Bonaparte's behalf, though the Military Depot had only scanty proof of their actions.

"St. Croix, you know everyone, do you not? They have all assured me that you are bosom beaux."

"Really?" Richard drawled and handed a cup to Lady Dorington and the other to Rose. "How are you Stykes? Recovered from last evening?"

Stykes, a thin young man who markedly resembled a ferret, nodded. "Far better than you, I'll wager. But how is it you have stolen a march on us and engaged the affections of Miss Maynwaring before any of us had even a glimpse of her lovely countenance?"

"Miss Maynwaring's and my betrothal is one of long-standing, arranged by our families since our nursery days. Out of respect for the recent death of her grandfather and my cousin, the official notice

47

was withheld until now." He looked over Stykes's shoulder as if he were searching for someone.

"Who are you looking for, St. Croix?" one of the other young bucks asked curiously.

"Trumble. Where Stykes is, can Trumble be far behind?"

This brought appreciative snickers from the other males. Neither Stykes nor Trumble were popular with them and they had no compunction about enjoying a jest at their expense.

A blond young man in a military uniform addressed Rose. "Since we have St. Croix's word that you have known him from infancy, you must tell us about this mystery man. He crops up from nowhere, wealthier than any man has a right to be, and steals the fairest new flower to grace London in many a Season. 'Tis only fair you tell us more of him."

Rose nearly panicked. What should she say? She drew on the scanty knowledge she had learned in Copter's office and improvised. "Well, you must know, we weren't really that well acquainted as children. Except at the usual family gatherings, we saw little of each other. After all, he was a boy, with a boy's interests. We did not live close to each other. I was in school in Bath and he resided in," here she had to pause. To cover the lapse, she sipped from the punch cup, "in Cornwall."

"Cornwall!" One of the bucks turned incredulous eyes on the elegantly dressed St. Croix. "I didn't realize they even spoke English there."

"I had good tutors," Richard replied caustically. "And I attended Eton as some of you well know."

" 'Tis true. My brother remembers you from Latin class. Said you had a habit of mimicking the teacher that sent them all in stitches. My brother is Robert Fitzwarren," the young man added.

"Of course I remember him," Richard smiled. Inwardly he groaned. Too much of his real background

48

was being dragged out. Sooner or later someone would remember they had a cousin who shared a class with him at Cambridge or a brother who was in the same command with him before Sir Michael had recruited him.

"With your permission, St. Croix, I should like to ask Miss Maynwaring for this set." The younger Fitzwarren held out his arm to Rose.

Richard nodded, and Rose took the young man's arm.

Lady Beresford commanded Richard's attention and admonished him to make himself available to the other young ladies hoping to dance. As her guest, he could hardly refuse, and he used the opportunity to further his wastrel image by dancing with every beautiful woman in the room and whispering flirtations in their ears.

Nor had Lady Dorington missed his actions. To her worldly eye, it appeared that St. Croix was going out of his way to make a spectacle of himself. She'd have a word with that young man before the night was out.

Richard escorted the two ladies into supper and saw to filling their plates from the huge buffet offered. When he returned, he was pleased to see Rose had selected a small table where no others could join them.

"Ah, private at last, or the closest thing that passes for it in this crush. How are you enjoying your first London ball, Rose? You certainly don't want for partners."

"Very much, thank you. Everything is so beautiful and gay. And you, my lord? Are you enjoying the evening?"

Richard immediately picked up on her using the polite form of address rather than his given name. Still, he had a part to play. "Immensely. Lord and Lady Beresford certainly have outdone themselves.

Just look at this repast. Lobster, quail's eggs, sorbet, everything to tease the palate."

"Yes, it certainly is delicious. Don't you think so, Aunt Bernie?"

Her aunt merely nodded.

I want to leave, Rose inwardly admitted. I want to run away from this place with its false smiles and fake manners. I wish I had never come and seen Richard flirting with pretty widows and preening like a peacock. Aloud, she added, "I fear I am unused to all the excitement. Would you mind if we left a bit early?"

"Aren't you well, Rose? If you feel ill, I shall send for the carriage immediately." Lady Dorington looked concerned.

Rose shook her head. "I'm not ill. I just feel— weary."

"It's all that dancing. I feared you overdid it a bit," Richard pronounced somewhat pompously. "However, if you can manage, I feel we should remain at least until midnight. After all, my dear, this is our first entry into society together. It would seem strange if we left too abruptly. Perhaps you would care to join me in the card room after supper? You could sit and play a few hands of silver loo. I'll back you."

"I'm not much one for cards." Rose took a bite of the pigeon pie on her plate.

Richard smiled at that. "Time you learned. Whist and silver loo are as much a social grace as dancing." He continued to override any further objections and, when the meal was over, escorted Rose into the Beresford card room across the hall from the main salon.

"Please, Richard, I would prefer to just watch." Rose refused a place at one of the tables.

"As you will, sweetheart." Richard placed a chair slightly to one side of his own. "We'll be playing All

Fours. Penny stakes, I believe Lady Beresford said."

The two other gentlemen at the table harrumphed at that. The other player, a dowager of ample proportions, gave an unladylike snort.

"Well, then, would you care to up the wager? No one need know outside of us." Richard smiled at the others.

"Make it a pound minimum," the dowager suggested and all agreed.

Richard waited while the woman dealt. As the player to her left, he examined his hand and compared it with the turned-up trump card. "I stand," he said and led his first card. He took the first trick, but after that it was down hill. It soon became obvious that he had fallen in with a group of sharps, and there wasn't much he could do about it. The new St. Croix wasn't downy enough to recognize the tactics they were using.

Rose picked up on the rules quickly and realized that Richard was losing heavily. Through it all, he kept up a cheerful, uncaring front, as if it were pennies and not hundreds of pounds he was losing. Finally she could watch no more.

"Richard." Rose laid a hand on his shoulder to get his attention. "Richard, Aunt Bernie must be ready to leave by now."

Richard heaved a huge sigh and tossed in his cards. "So be it. I fear I must leave you, sirs, lady. Thank you for a most interesting game." He hid the sarcasm in his remark, since it had become clear from the second hand that these three worked together to fleece an unwary player. Ah, well, it would add to his reputation, he thought.

The drive back to Park House was spent in discussing the various personages that had been at the fete. It was only after Richard had seen them inside and Rose had said her good nights that Lady Dorington insisted he join her in the drawing room for a few moments. Once they were private, she turned on him, anger sparking from her eyes.

"Just what is the meaning of your conduct, young man?" she demanded.

"I beg your pardon, Lady Dorington. To what are you referring? Certainly nothing I did tonight was beyond acceptable behavior."

"Do not bandy words with me, St. Croix. I spent half the night hearing of your exploits. Did you think that your attendance at Amelia Wessex's and like establishments would not be noted? Are you such a fool that you think you can snub your nose at proprieties and still remain in society's good graces? Already there are rumors of you having a mistress, several for that matter. Are these rumors true? Is Rose engaged to a philanderer?"

"Lady Dorington, what activities I indulge in outside of Miss Maynwaring's company is none of your concern, as you well know. I will not tolerate your interference in my affairs. And I will thank you not to mention any of this to your niece." He emphasized his words by slapping his gloves across the palm of his hand.

"Do you think Rose does not know? She has eyes and ears."

"I think Rose has the good sense to consider the source. Lady Dorington, if she and I are content in our arrangement, who are you to poke and prod? Rose is of legal age and can wed where she chooses. She has chosen me. You can either accept the wisdom of her choice or not, as you will. But, you cannot change it.

"I suggest," Richard softened his tone, "that you honor her decision and have a little faith. It matters not what society thinks as long as we are pleased."

"These rumors have already wounded her." Lady Dorington countered. "If the accounts are only half true, you are well on your way to ruination. I will not have you drag Rose with you. She has had enough pain in her life."

"Pain? How is that? I was under the impression that she had been well, if moderately, taken care of."

Lady Dorington sighed and gestured for him to have a seat on the settee. Perhaps if he knew a little of Rose's background, he would understand how uncomfortable the notoriety he was causing was for her. "You already know the unfortunate circumstances of her birth. St. Croix, her grandfather, paid for her upkeep and education, but he never even saw her after the day she was born. I had married Sir Oliver Dorington and had gone with him to his embassy post in Spain. I asked St. Croix several times to let me raise Rose, but he refused. Rose was subjected to the slights and hurts of the other schoolgirls because of the circumstances of her birth. I know those hurts cut deeper than she admits. She fears that her illegitimacy already puts her beyond the pale, as far as society is concerned. Your behavior adds to her anxiety."

Richard refrained from comment for some moments. Here was a devil of a turnup. But hurt her he must, for there was no alternative. For the good of England he must enter France and collect the information about Napoleon's movements.

"I thank you for your confidences, Lady Dorington," he drawled. "But, I fear you are overly concerned. The Viscountess St. Croix Rose will be accepted anywhere. She must learn to have a thicker skin and ignore the barbs that are thrown her way." He rose. "Now, I must be off. I did not have a chance to tell Rose, but I must be out of town for a few days. Business affairs, you understand. By the by, we have been invited to Lord Tarasford's house party next weekend. The Prince of Wales will be there, so I was certain you would not mind my accepting on the behalf of all three of us. Lady Tarasford is expecting you on Thursday afternoon in time for tea. If you need anything, Mr. Copter has been instructed to provide for you. I'm afraid I shan't be able to visit with Rose before the house party, so I shall meet you all there. Good evening, Lady Dorington."

Before she could retort, Richard had taken up his hat and was out the door.

"Well, of all the gall!" she said indignantly, startling the butler who had come in to see if she needed anything.

"My lady?" he asked.

"That, Smethwick, is the most cocksure jackanapes it has ever been my misfortune to encounter!"

"Yes, my lady," the butler said in totally neutral tones. "Will there be anything else?"

Recollecting whom she was addressing, Lady Dorington gave a little dismissing wave with her handkerchief. "Nothing else, Smethwick, except to inform the staff that Miss Maynwaring and I will be out of town this weekend."

"Very good, my lady." Smethwick backed out of the room.

Chapter Five

"WELCOME, LADY DORINGTON, Miss Maynwaring. Welcome to Tarasford Hall." Sir Michael greeted the ladies in the entry of his ancestral home.

Rose looked around appreciatively at the marble floor and Italian balustrade that ran along the double staircase and gallery above. At the base of each set of stairs a footman stood, wearing the red-and-black livery of the house. On the wall below the gallery, the Tarasford crest was carved into a huge piece of black-veined marble. Overall, it was an impressive sight.

"Your house is beautiful," Rose said to Lady Tarasford after the introductions were made.

"Thank you, my dear. It's a bit of a hodgepodge of styles. Are you interested in architecture, Miss Maynwaring?"

"Yes. I find so much history in the buildings." Rose smiled at the other woman. She followed her aunt and Lady Tarasford up the left set of stairs and into the east wing.

"His Royal Highness will be occupying the first floor of this wing. All the other guests will be with you on the second. I've assigned Tillie to you and Miss Maynwaring, Lady Dorington. Richard told me you haven't had time to find a maid yet. Tillie is studying under my own maid, Rachel."

"We were so delighted that you could come. When Richard told us of his engagement, Sir Michael absolutely insisted he introduce us. By the by, Richard has the room two doors down from yours." Lady Tarasford kept up a stream of conversation as they moved along yet another gallery and up a wide wooden stair to the next level.

"Have you known the viscount long?" Rose asked.

"Since he first joined the service, about eight years or so. He served under my husband as a lieutenant. We are so pleased with his recent good fortune."

Does that include his intended bride? Rose asked herself as they continued down the hall.

"Lady Dorington, this will be your room." Their hostess opened the heavy oak door and preceded them in. She turned around to face the two other ladies. "I hope you will find it comfortable. The bellpull is next to the bed, should you need anything."

Obviously the room had been prepared with comfort in mind. A fire blazed in the hearth and the bed was covered with a down-filled mulberry-and-pink spread.

"Most comfortable, thank you." Aunt Bernie looked around the room appreciatively.

"Miss Maynwaring will be right across the hall. I thought the two of you would like to be close."

"Very considerate of you, Lady Tarasford," Aunt Bernie again thanked her.

"Athena, please. Even though I've lived in this country for nearly twenty-five years, I still find some of the etiquette a bit stuffy. We are more relaxed in Virginia."

"Only if you will reciprocate and call me Bernie." Lady Dorington chuckled at the look of consternation in Athena Tarasford's eyes. "It's short for Bernadette. My mother was of a religious bent."

"Alas, I am just a plain Rose among these exotic blooms of names," Rose joked.

"Nonsense, I always thought my sister showed re-markable good sense in your name. You do realize you came very close to being christened Stephina Hagar?"

"A rose by any other name would smell as sweet." Richard's voice drew their eyes to where he stood in the doorway.

"Eavesdropping, St. Croix?" Lady Tarasford arched an eyebrow.

"Not intentionally, I do assure you. I happened to be passing and heard the conversation." Richard smiled at the three ladies.

Athena took Rose's arm and led her back into the hall. "I didn't know you had arrived, Richard. I was just showing Rose to her chamber." She paused and studied Richard's mud-splattered form. "Is that any way to present yourself?" she said in chastising tones.

"I was just on my way to my room when I heard you in here. I do apologize, but my appearance is the result of a bang-up wager. I placed a bet that I could make it from Croydon to here in less than two hours, and I won! Dirty business though." He frowned down at his splotched breeches.

Rose looked at him with amazement. It took three-and-a-half hours to reach Tarasford Hall from the small town of Croydon by coach. Richard must have raced recklessly across the countryside to win his bet. At every turn he seemed to be taking outrageous chances only to win a few guineas. What manner of man had she become involved with? Was her future to be filled with uncertainties based on the turn of a card?

"Well, I'm delighted to see you," Lady Tarasford was saying. "Have you seen Sir Michael yet? I know he had some things he wished to discuss with you. You should find him in his study, hiding from all the hullabaloo."

"Lady Athena, you have such a colorful way of speaking. Do all Americans talk in such a descriptive way?" Richard teased.

"Get on with you now. Rose, this will be your room." Her hostess opened the door across the hall from Lady Dorington's.

Richard bowed to them. "Rose, it's good to see you looking so lovely. Most women would look drawn and harried after such a long trip from town, but you look as fresh as the dew-kissed morn. Shall I see you later and give you a tour of the grounds?"

"You may join us later for tea." Lady Tarasford forestalled Rose. "That is about an hour from now. Until then, I'm certain Rose would like to freshen up." Athena Tarasford stood back to let him pass.

With another wicked grin, Richard made his exit.

"Supper will be informal this evening. Most of the guests will not arrive until tomorrow. His Royal Highness has promised to be here for the ball in the evening. Have you met the Prince of Wales yet?"

Rose shook her head. "I haven't had the pleasure."

"Ah, well, I'll make a point of it tomorrow night. Albeit, an introduction to Prinny can be a mixed blessing." She gave a little giggle. "He's gotten a bit large, you know. Creaks, poor man. It's the corsets he wears." Lady Tarasford went about the bedchamber, checking the grate and pulling the curtains back farther to allow more of the feeble February sunlight into the room. "Do you ride, Rose? If so, the stable is at your disposal. I haven't organized any formal rides since most of the ladies coming are not of that bent."

"Yes, I do, thank you. Perhaps tomorrow morning? I enjoy an early canter."

"Do you? So do I. Unfortunately, I won't be able to join you tomorrow, but perhaps we could Sunday."

"I would like that very much."

"Fine then. I'll see you for tea."

Rose watched as her hostess left the room. Two footmen brought in her trunks, followed by a young maid with apple cheeks and a cheerful smile.

"I'm Tillie, miss. Would you like me to unpack for you?"

"Yes, thank you Tillie." Rose went over to the fireplace and warmed her hands. Then she took off her wine velvet cape and handed it over to the maid. She watched as Tillie began to put away the contents of the trunks. How Madame Vereaux was able to finish these gowns so quickly, I can't imagine, Rose thought to herself as each garment was removed from its tissue and either hung in the wardrobe or placed in the cherry-wood dresser. There were three morning gowns, three afternoon dresses, the carriage ensemble she now wore, a forest green riding habit, and three evening gowns, not to mention the silk and linen unmentionables and hose, shoes, reticules, hats, gloves, and other paraphernalia necessary to maintain the proper image of the future Viscountess St. Croix.

But, do I really want to be a viscountess? Rose mused. Do I really want to spend my life with Richard? Certainly when we are together he behaves in a manner any woman would find gratifying, but the rumors, the long absences, are they indications of what I can expect? And what about his gambling? Even the St. Croix money will run out someday at the rate he is losing his portion. Does he plan to dip into my inheritance to cover his debts? Is that why he is marrying me?

But, what other future do I have? And what of Aunt Bernie? Her kindness to me deserves more than for me to throw this opportunity away. Other women have married in a similar manner. They seem to live full, productive lives.

"Which would you care to wear for tea, miss?" Tillie's voice broke into Rose's thoughts.

"The lavender, I suppose." Rose indicated the cashmere dress hanging on the door of the wardrobe.

"Very good, miss. I'll take it down to the pantry and press it after I stop by Lady Dorington's room. The boys will be bringing your bath in a moment. By the time you've finished bathing, the dress will be ready."

"That will be fine, Tillie."

Tillie waited until the large copper tub had been positioned before the fire and a privacy screen set up to shield it from drafts. She then placed Rose's toiletries on a stool next to the tub, along with a snowy white bath sheet. Finally she added lilac oil to the water and stirred it around a bit. "Bath's ready, miss."

Once Rose was safely ensconced in the warm water, Tillie took up the dress and left the room.

Richard found Sir Michael in his study at the back of the house. The older man was bending over documents spread on a long table in the center of the room.

"The latest report from La Havre. Bonaparte's up to something, there's no doubt. He's hated our continued control of the seas and chafed under the terms of the Treaty of Amiens. The question is, what? The sooner you get over there, my boy, the better." He handed Richard one of the parchments.

The viscount perused the missive and then handed it back to his superior. "Whatever it is, it can mean no good for us."

"There is such a feeling of distrust even among our own agents, they will not turn over their information to anyone but you. I don't suppose there is any way we could speed up your wedding?" Sir Michael asked hopefully.

"I don't really see how, sir. The proprieties must be observed. Otherwise, it might call attention to me, the kind we wish to avoid."

"You're right, of course. Pity we can't think of some reason that the popinjay St. Croix would leave for the Continent quickly. Some usual reason, creditors or heartbroken, that sort of thing." Sir Michael paced the length of his study.

"Hmm," Richard murmured, then spoke up. "Creditors are unlikely, since all the world believes that I inherited a fortune from the old viscount. But there just might be a way."

"Have you thought of something St. Croix?"

"Perhaps. But it will have to happen this weekend, here, at your house. And it might ruin Lady Tarasford's ball."

"Never mind that. Athena has been my confidante for over twenty-five years. She'll understand and help."

Later that evening, Tillie led Rose to the main parlor where the family and guests gathered before going into supper. Part of the Italian section of the house, the room was kept warm by a large porcelain stove worked with garlands of painted flowers and cherubs.

The rest of the room was done in shades of blue and gold, with cream walls and frescoes depicting the four seasons. To one side was a pianoforte, also painted cream. Lady Tarasford was sitting at the keyboard chatting with some of her guests. She came over as she saw Rose enter the room.

"Your aunt sent word she would be down directly," her hostess said after greeting her.

"I know. I stopped by Aunt Bernie's room before I came." Rose looked around expecting to see Richard.

"I'm afraid St. Croix hasn't made an appearance yet, either." Lady Tarasford interpreted her look. "He was discussing some business with my husband and, I'm sure, forgot about the time. As you can see, even Sir Michael is not present, and he's the host!"

She accompanied this statement with a little laugh. "Come, let me introduce you to the others."

The guest list seemed to be weighted heavily in favor of the military, Rose observed as she was introduced to a second admiral. They were names she was vaguely familiar with from the tabloids, but having just come from Winchester, she knew little of the power these men held.

"Dreadfully sorry to be so late," Richard apologized to Lady Tarasford as he entered, "but I wagered my valet he couldn't tie my neck cloth properly without ruining at least three. Zounds, but he did it and this is the result." Richard gently patted the froth of lace at his throat.

Rose realized she was staring at him. To lay money on the least little thing was bad enough, but to bet with one's servants, that was beyond the pale in her opinion.

Further conversation was curtailed by the announcement of the meal. Sir Michael escorted his wife to the dining room, followed by Lady Dorington on the arm of a widowed general. Richard took Rose's arm and led her into Lady Tarasford's "informal meal."

What will the banquet be like tomorrow night if this is a casual supper? Rose thought wryly. There were eight courses, plus removes, and a choice of three desserts. The appropriate wine was served with each course and Rose found she had to put her hand over her glass to keep the wine steward from filling it too often. It wouldn't do for her to become light-headed.

After the meal, the ladies withdrew to the main parlor again where they sat and gossiped. Each took a turn playing the pianoforte. Rose was seated at the keyboard rendering a Mozart piece when the men returned from their cigars and port.

"You never told me you were an accomplished pianist," Richard commented when she had finished.

"Aren't all young ladies expected to play and sing? At least, at the Bath Academy, that is what Mrs. Rys insisted."

"Really? I'm just beginning to realize how little I know about you. Perhaps you'd care to see the paintings in the gallery and talk a bit?"

Here was the opportunity that Rose had been waiting for. Perhaps they could now have a serious discussion about their future. "I should like that."

"Then let's slip away before our hostess or your aunt notice." He guided her to the door.

The main drawing room was on the first floor at the top of the right staircase. Richard drew Rose along the balcony overlooking the entry and into the door opposite. This was a long, wide corridor well lit by tapers. Along both walls was a line of paintings, portraits of the Tarasford family dating back to fourteen hundred. At the end closest to them, Sir Michael and Lady Tarasford peered down. Rose liked the painting. Sir Michael stood behind his seated wife with his hand resting lightly on her shoulder. It was a warm and intimate portrayal.

"Do you think we'll be as fortunate as the Tarasfords?" Rose asked, turning to face Richard.

He had been admiring the way the candles caused her hair to sparkle with red highlights, reminding him of their first encounter. From his position behind her, he could smell the sweet fragrance of her skin. It took all his control not to trace the gentle curve of her ivory neck with his fingertip. Instead, when she turned around, he leaned casually forward, resting his hand on the wall between the paintings.

"Things were not always so easy between them," he said seriously. "Athena is an American. They met when Sir Michael was sent to Canada. He was her enemy. Their love was rented and torn in those days.

63

Such circumstances either temper love like steel, or destroy it. For it to survive, that kind of love takes a great deal of effort. Are you willing to make the effort, Rose?" He fixed her with his sultry blue eyes.

Rose felt as if she had been pinned to the wall like a butterfly in a collection. What did he mean? Was he offering more than the casual relationship she had thought he wanted? He overpowered her with his eyes, those eyes that seemed to reach into her soul for its most hidden secrets. "It is the kind of love all women dream of," she finally breathed. "If such were offered to me, yes, I'd fight tooth and nail to keep it." She inhaled sharply as his mouth came down on hers.

All reason fled as she felt herself plummeting into the exquisite abyss of his kiss. She had little experience with such things, and the maelstrom of emotions that his embrace stirred in her was frightening. She struggled to rally her sanity and, finally, her will asserted itself over her heart.

"Please . . . Don't." She put her palms on his chest and tried to push him away.

"Why not? Do you find me distasteful? I think not." Richard gave a little self-satisfied smile.

"I don't know you," she said. "Each time we are together, you are different. When we first met, I felt we had much in common, but lately, you seem more concerned with the fold of your cravat than getting to know me. I am not some foolish girl who will sigh and simper to build your male ego. And, by the way," she said, wanting to deflate his conceit, "that coat is atrocious."

"Atrocious! I suppose a little nobody like you from Winchester knows about fashion?" Richard's rising passion, so abruptly squelched, turned into frustrated anger. "As for getting to know you, I already do. It wasn't hard to determine that you are a mercenary female who is willing to enter a marriage she

64

loathes simply because of the wealth and prestige it will bring. Get used to the idea of my embraces, sweeting, because, once we are wed, you will have no choice. Remember the old viscount's stipulations."

"You said you would not push to have an heir immediately! Are you now going back on your word?" Rose hotly demanded.

"I've changed my mind," Richard said coldly. Damned woman, why is she doing this? Damn Sir Michael for forcing me to keep these barriers between us! And damn me for being a romantic idiot! He stepped back from Rose. "Whatever you are, Rose, you are mine. And you will do well to remember that I do with mine what I please." With that he turned on his heel and left her.

Rose slept badly that night. Her dreams disintegrated into nightmares as she saw herself dancing with Richard in a beautiful ballroom only to look into his face and see his handsome countenance change into the grotesque visage of a demon.

When she awoke, she was determined to get away from the house with its accompanying social obligations for a while. Hadn't Lady Tarasford offered her the use of the stable? An early morning ride would clear the last shreds of her dreams away. She rang for Tillie and hopped out of bed.

The little maid appeared while Rose was finishing her toilette. She carried a silver tray with the usual morning chocolate. "You're an early riser, miss."

"Thank you for the chocolate, Tillie. Would you send a message to the stables that I should like to go for a ride shortly?"

"Certainly, miss. But don't ride toward the village. There's a rumor that a mad dog was seen in its streets last night."

Rose blanched at the thought of rabies. "Did it bite anyone?"

65

"Not that I heard. But you should be safe enough on the estate. The village is a good two miles from here."

With that, Tillie laid out the accessories that went with her riding habit. "I'll send word to Timmins."

After the maid had left, Rose took up the delicate china cup and carried it over to the vanity where Tillie had left her hat and gloves. She took sips from the cup as she finished pinning her hair and setting the miniature beaver cap on her head. When the ends of the long scarf that swathed its crown fell gracefully down her back, Rose secured the hat firmly to her head with a long hat pin.

"That should do," she said with satisfaction at her reflection. She smoothed the fitted waist of the green velvet jacket one more time and left for the stables.

A middle-aged man, his sideburns and huge mustache salted with gray, was barking orders to the grooms and stable boys. Rose approached him slowly. "Mr. Timmins?"

"Aye, miss. You be the one what wants to go for a ride?" He looked her over carefully, then turned to the nearest lackey. "Put a lady's saddle on Arabella." Turning back to Rose he explained. "She's a pretty-behaved lil' darlin' with a spring in her step and sauciness in her spirit that makes her a joy to ride."

"Thank you, Timmins. I'm sure she'll be fine."

Arabella proved to be exactly what the head groom had promised. She was a dainty dapple gray mare with a shimmering white mane and tail. Rose mounted her easily.

"Seth will attend you, miss." Timmins indicated an already mounted groom.

Rose nodded, knowing that for her to ride unaccompanied, even on the estate, was unacceptable. She turned Arabella around and headed down the path that led from the stables into the estate park.

The air was chilly with the last bite of winter and

her breath came out in white vapors. Once beyond the stable yard, she urged Arabella into a canter, taking pleasure in the smooth, rocking rhythm of the gait.

They continued until the path forked. Rose pulled to a stop and called back to the groom. "Where do these lead, Seth?"

"Tarasford village is to the left, miss. The right goes into the hunting preserve." The groom drew level with Rose.

"We'll go right, then." Rose turned Arabella's head and proceeded into the deeper woods at a slower pace.

A silence hung over the huge trees, disturbed only by the clop of the horses' hooves. Rose spotted a fallow deer among the great trunks, but the creature bolted before she could approach. Light barely penetrated, shut out by the branches of firs and pines. Someone had kept the path clear of overhanging brush, but the trail grew fainter the deeper into the wood she went. The gloom of the place began to oppress her.

"I think we should turn back," she called to Seth who rode behind her. "Lady Tarasford has plans for later this morning and I must change."

Seth urged his horse off the path so that Rose could turn Arabella around and pass him. Once past the groom, Rose once again urged the mare into a brisk canter.

She leaned into the horse, letting herself enjoy the feeling of freedom riding gave her. Even as she urged Arabella into a gallop, she heard a loud report. Something whizzed by her left shoulder and she felt a hot streak of pain. Arabella, frightened by the shot, stumbled and Rose went tumbling to the ground.

"Miss, miss, are ye all right?" Seth hurried up to her and dismounted.

"I don't know," Rose said, dazed. She had managed

to roll to a sitting position. Now she examined her left arm. The bullet had torn through the slight puffing of the sleeve of her riding coat, grazing her arm.

"Are ye hurt bad, miss?" Seeing Rose shake her head, Seth continued. "Must be a poacher. I'll tell Perkins, the gamekeeper, when we get back. Can ye ride miss?"

"I think so. It's really nothing. Just a scratch."

"Then I'll go fetch Arabella. She'd not have gone far."

While the groom went in search of the horse, Rose rested and collected herself. Slight as the wound was, she had felt a wave of nausea when she realized she had been shot. She put her head between her knees to fight off the rising faintness.

By the time the groom returned with the mare, Rose was feeling better. Her arm hurt, as if it had been badly bruised, and she realized she must have injured it more when she fell. She tentatively moved her shoulder, then slowly swung her left arm back and forth. Finding the pain bearable, she remounted Arabella with the help of Seth. The pain settled down to a dull throb on the ride back to the main house.

"If ye don't mind goin' in through the west wing, miss, you'll find Mrs. Wainwright in the distillery. She should look at your arm, miss. She's right good at patchin' up the scrapes we get around here." Seth indicated an ancient oak door in the Norman tower.

"Thank you, but it's barely noticeable now."

"Right, miss. But she makes a salve what helps make hurts stop hurtin'. Keeps cuts from turnin' putrid, too. 'Tis better to be safe, miss. Let her look at it."

"Very well, I will. And thank you for your concern, Seth."

"Yer welcome, miss." Seth helped her dismount and took the mare's reins. He remounted his own horse and set off in the direction of the stables.

Rose started for the door when she saw a male figure move across the lawn on the north side of the tower. She recognized Richard and started around the corner to hail him. She stopped dead in her tracks, just behind a barren forsythia bush and stared at what Richard was carrying.

Richard shifted the rifle in his hand to his shoulder. He looked around, causing Rose to sink closer to the tower. Then, furtively it seemed to Rose, he slipped through a small portal.

Chapter Six

Deep in thought, Rose returned to the side door that would take her into the distillery room. The pungent odors of the small, stone room assailed her nostrils as she pushed open the door. Lavender mixed with lemon, anise, fennel, mint, and a hundred other smells from years of preparing the medicines, scents, and flavorings for the household. The flagstone floor was swept clean and the rock walls were whitewashed and scrupulously clean. One entire end wall had shelves reaching up to the ceiling, all crammed with clay pots, bottles, and tins of the commodities made there. A short, stout woman in a mop hat and white apron was carefully placing small salve pots on the lowest shelf.

"Mrs. Wainwright?" Rose said, hesitantly.

The woman straightened and, seeing Rose's torn sleeve and still pale complexion, hurried over to the door. "What happened, miss? I'll send for Lady Tarasford right away." She helped Rose to one of the small stools.

"Please don't. She has enough to do with the Prince of Wales arrival this afternoon. I am fine, really. It was just that the groom insisted I should see you for fear the scratch may fester. I don't wish to upset the household over such a small matter."

"And how did this happen, miss?" Mrs. Wainwright was already examining the torn buckram of the riding jacket and the broken skin beneath it.

"A poacher I suppose. A stray shot. I don't really know. I think I did more damage when I fell from Arabella than the bullet did."

"Poachers! On Sir Michael's land! He needs to be told at once, miss."

"The groom said he would tell the gamekeeper. I'm certain Sir Michael will be informed."

Mrs. Wainwright began helping Rose out of the riding jacket. Rose winced with pain. Her shoulder had become stiff and sore and it hurt to move it.

"I'll send for Tillie. She be takin' care of ye, ain't she, miss?" Seeing Rose's nod, Mrs. Wainwright went to the door and summoned a lackey to fetch the little maid.

The astringent stung, and Rose sucked in her breath. While the wound was being cleansed, Tillie burst in.

"What happened, miss? Are you all right?" The maid hurried over to Rose.

"I'm fine, Tillie. I just got a scratch when I fell from my horse."

"Praise the Lord, miss. I thought the mad dog had got you."

Mrs. Wainwright turned a disapproving frown on the maid. "Be still, girl, until I finish with Miss Maynwaring. Then ye take her up to her room and draw a hot bath for her and put her down for a nice rest. Fetch her a toddy to help her sleep a bit."

"No, please, I'd rather have tea." Rose began to feel like an infant being tended by her nanny.

"Very well, tea, but with a spot of rum in it. It will help ye rest, miss, and do ye no harm." Mrs. Wainwright blotted Rose's arm and applied some of the salve. "There'll be a bruise by this evenin', miss."

"Oh, miss, your beautiful gown! The bruise will

show." Tillie nearly wrung her hands in distress at Rose's appearance being marred by the accident. "And His Royal Highness coming!"

Mrs. Wainwright went over to her shelves and rummaged through them, emerging triumphantly with a small tin. "This should do the trick. Remember old Lady Baxter, the one what was so vain?"

"Sir Michael's aunt? Aye, of course I do. She wore all that paint and powder."

"The last time she visited, she had me make up a batch of that stuff she smears on her face. There's a bit of it in this tin. You can paint over Miss Maynwaring's bruise so it won't show." She turned to Rose. "It ain't like yer paintin' yer face or turnin' hussy, miss."

Rose tried hard not to laugh. "Thank you, Mrs. Wainwright. I assure you, we will use the cosmetic with the utmost discretion. And thank you again for attending to my hurts. I feel much better already." She began to put on the jacket. Tillie hurried to help her. Dressed, Rose headed for the door, followed by the maid carrying the medicine and paint.

Back in her room, Rose donned a wrapper and seated herself on the slipper chair to await the arrival of her bath and tea. She realized that she hadn't eaten breakfast yet, and she asked Tillie to include a bite to eat when she brought the beverage.

While she waited, Rose thought back to the sight of Richard carrying the rifle. There couldn't be a connection, she thought. He was angry with me last night, but he certainly wouldn't try to kill me. Moral reasons aside, he cannot inherit the money until we are married. There would be no profit in eliminating me now. She shook her head as if to clear the morbid thoughts from her brain. Could it have been a warning? Richard is, or was, a military man. I presume he must be a good shot. Perhaps he never meant to hit me. Perhaps it was a warning, just as his actions last night were a warning. Oh, what have I gotten myself into? I cannot marry a man I am so uncertain of. I must call the whole thing off.

She leaned back against the chair and closed her eyes. Thoughts of the previous evening brought back the kiss he had forced upon her. She blushed, realizing that part of her had enjoyed that embrace, even desired it to be repeated. What is this man doing to my peace of mind? Am I so like my mother that I allow emotions to overthrow common sense? But I cannot let it overwhelm me. I must end this relationship.

Richard finished cleaning the rifle at the table in Sir Michael's gun room and carefully replaced it in the rack. An interesting piece, he thought, as he admired the fine bore and ornate etchings on the barrel.

"There's our local hero!" a masculine voice boomed from the gun-room door. "St. Croix, I never knew you to be such a devilish good shot." Lord Admiral Fitzsimmons entered the room, followed by most of the other male guests and Sir Michael.

"B'gads, men, I have no idea how I managed it," Richard lied. "Usually, I'm a mile off my mark. Pity no one was about to take a wager on the shot. And the cropper is that the devilish backlash bruised my shoulder. I fear I shall have to take to my bed for the next several days. Would anyone care to wager how long it will take me to recuperate?"

"What, and miss Prinny? Nonsense. You'll just have to bear up, old man." Sir Michael slapped him on the shoulder in encouragement.

"Gadzooks, Sir Michael, do you wish to cripple me for life?" Richard winced and grabbed his shoulder as if in great pain.

"Nonetheless, you killed that rabid mongrel with one shot. Say what you might, the villagers are singing your praises all over the countryside. If you hadn't taken him down just when you did, the mangy cur would have gotten that child."

"Yes, it was rather brave of me, wasn't it?" Richard removed his snuffbox and took a pinch, making a great show of shaking back the lace at his wrist and flicking the box open with one hand. "I do believe I need a drop of brandy. The exigencies of the morning, you understand."

"Good man," the lord admiral said, "we'll join you."

As they drank the libation, the talk turned to the unseasonably fine weather they had been having, and finally, to politics. Each man had an opinion and, as the glasses were refilled, felt compelled to express it.

"What do you think St. Croix? What of this Bonaparte fellow?" Sir Michael asked, his face as bland as porridge.

"Why, sir, I don't think of him at all. I fear, it is difficult enough for me to concentrate on the play of my cards. Certainly, such thoughts are more rewarding. I mean, dash it all, what can I do about Napoleon? Damned nuisance, if you ask me, but otherwise, of no account. But a properly played card, why, a man's entire fortune can rest on such considerations."

His response brought snickers from the younger men present and a mumbled "damned wastrel" from the lord admiral. Richard had sufficiently squelched any notions of his heroism in that quarter.

A footman entered with a message for Sir Michael.

"Gentlemen, His Royal Highness's advance party has arrived. Prinny will be here within the hour. I suggest we prepare ourselves accordingly."

"Here, here!" several of the men cheered and held out their glasses to be refilled.

"Michael, what am I to do? He's brought Mrs.

Fitzherbert with him." Lady Tarasford whispered to her husband as they waited in line to receive the Prince. "His man of chambers told me."

Richard, who happened to be standing on the other side of Lady Tarasford, heard the remark and sympathized. It was an awkward situation to have the royal mistress in the same house with so many sympathizers of the queen. The lord admiral, for one, he knew to be one of the Fitzherbert's detractors. But there were just as many who regarded the lady as the prince's real wife, witnessed by the many children she had produced for him. Having her here might just aid in the plan he and Sir Michael had hatched.

The royal coach drew up before the door and the footmen jumped down to lower the steps and adjust the carpet path for the convenience of the royal personage. Rose, who stood farther down the line and thus closer to the door, was amused to see how everyone jockeyed for position to be near the carriage. To her surprise, Richard relinquished his spot and came to stand beside her and her aunt. The position was quickly filled by the lord admiral's curvaceous daughter.

"Lady Tarasford is in a quandry. Mrs. Fitzherbert arrives with His Royal Highness," Richard whispered to Lady Dorington and Rose.

Lady Dorington snapped her parasol open and placed it on her shoulder. "What a faradiddle over nothing. Royalty does not conform to the same rules as we mere mortals.

"I have heard that he really is married to her but because of the royal charter, it is not recognized as legal. Parliament would not hear of a morganatic marriage for him."

Rose whispered back to her aunt. "I think it would be awful to love a man as much as she must and never be able to marry him."

"Hush, child, His Royal Highness is leaving his coach," Lady Dorington admonished Rose.

All eyes turned to the open carriage door. Sir Michael approached the coach and assisted the Prince to alight. the double line of guests bowed deeply; the ladies sinking down into low curtsies. From the corner of her eye, Rose saw the prince reach back in the coach and help a woman down the steps. Mrs. Fitzherbert, Rose thought, and watched curiously as the woman came to stand beside the prince. She was not much younger than the prince himself, and her figure could only be described as running to plump. Her face was kind, reminding Rose that she was rumored to be tremendously motherly in her dealings with the prince and their offspring.

At the Prince command, all rose, and the royal party began their progression along the line and into the house. The prince merely nodded and bowed, not stopping until he had reached the doors and was escorted inside. The crowd broke up then and followed. By the time Rose reached the entry, the prince's party had already been escorted to their rooms.

Now is my chance to tell Richard that I wish to end this fiasco of our engagement, she thought, trying to get St. Croix's attention. No amount of money is worth my life. Unfortunately, with all the milling about, she could not gain his notice.

"What ails you child?" Lady Dorington asked, seeing Rose's attempts.

"Aunt, I wish to have a few words in private with the viscount. But it is impossible in this crush to gain his attention."

"Is it so urgent it cannot wait? I fear, now that the Prince has arrived, everyone will be rushing hither and yon to please the royal personage. Perhaps this evening, when you are dancing. See, Sir Michael has already singled out St. Croix to attend to some little detail. There he is leading him off. I fear whatever it is, Rose, it must wait."

Sir Michael pulled Richard into his study. "I only have a moment, lad, but I wanted to tell you everything is set in motion. What a turn up Prinny's presence always makes. But, there has been a minor complication you should be aware of. One of the grooms reported a poacher on the premises. It seems that your Miss Maynwaring went riding this morning and very nearly caught a stray bullet."

"Rose was shot?" Richard felt the anxiety rise in him. "But I just saw her. She seemed perfectly fine."

"Shot at, boy. A random ball, no more. The groom said it grazed her arm and spooked her horse so that she fell. I wonder at her not saying anything. Simply had Mrs. Wainwright patch her up and went about her business. Said she didn't want to disturb the household in its preparations for the prince. Quite a girl, that."

Richard was still trying to digest the news that Rose had been injured. "Why didn't she say something to me? Even a graze can be painful. The shock alone must have been overwhelming."

"It seems to me you have more in that girl than you bargained for, St. Croix. She's got pluck, and that's a rare quality in females these days. See that you don't lose her." This last sounded like a military command.

"Easier said than done, sir. This character St. Croix that we've created is everything Rose finds abhorrent."

"After tonight, you will be assured of her. She seems an intelligent young woman. Once this is all over, you have my permission to explain everything.

But not until the mission has been accomplished. The fewer people who know, the safer you will be in France."

Richard nodded. "I understand, but it isn't easy, sir."

Sir Michael harrumphed a bit. "Duty seldom is, Richard."

Rose donned the aquamarine gown Madame Vereaux had made up especially for this gala. When the dressmaker had heard that the Regent Prince would be present, she once again became inspired and had her staff whip up the frock Rose now wore in record time. It was very simple in design, following madame's decision to dress Rose *a la classique*. The sleeves fell off the shoulder and were slit to the elbow. The raised waist was drawn together with a golden cord that crossed between her breasts and ended in small bows at the top of the sleeves.

As Rose examined her appearance in the mirror, she noticed that the bruised shoulder still looked yellowish with the concealing paint. She had Tillie fetch a gold tissue shawl Madame Vereaux had designed for another gown and draped it over the injured shoulder, imitating a Roman toga she had once seen in a drawing.

"Oh, miss, that looks right fine," Tillie cooed when she saw the result. "Just let me put a couple of stitches in it to hold the shawl in place, and you'll look like one of them Roman goddesses."

Rose had to admit that the addition of the shawl added a certain uniqueness to the dress. Her shoulder still ached dully, but it was bearable and Rose wasn't about to miss her chance to meet the Prince Regent.

"We're all to be assembled before His Royal Highness makes his entrance, Tillie. So I suppose I had better go down. I'll stop by my aunt's room. We can make our entrance together." Rose drew on the white kidskin opera gloves and adjusted the gold bracelet she wore over the leather. Next she picked up the St. Croix betrothal ring and slipped it on. People would think it strange if she appeared not wearing it this evening. She had already decided to give it back to Richard at the first opportunity. That done, she crossed the hall and knocked on her aunt's door.

"Come in," Lady Dorington called.

"It's just me, Aunt Bernie. Are you ready to go down?"

Lady Dorington took up her fan and lorgnette. "Indeed I am. That gown looks absolutely fetching. Mind you, Rose, the prince is notorious for cornering pretty women. Be careful when you are around him."

"Surely he would do nothing so untoward with Mrs. Fitzherbert present."

Lady Dorington shook her head. "One never knows what Prinny will do. Now, if you are ready, let us go down."

They left her room and started along the hall to the stairs when Richard joined them.

"Ah, we are all assembled. Now we can make our entrance together like the devoted couple we are," he remarked gaily. His eyes took in every point of Rose's appearance. "I must say, for a moment I thought Diana had emerged from her lunar home to grace the gathering tonight, so magically beautiful you do look, Rose."

"Why thank you, St. Croix, for that pretty speech." Rose tried hard not to let her anger with him show in her voice.

They made their way down the stairs to the first level where the gallery opened up into yet another set of wide steps leading down into the oval shaped ballroom of Tarasford Hall. Crystal chandeliers and strategically placed wall mirrors threw back the light of a thousand candles. Already ladies and gentlemen were dancing, glittering under the golden light with their jewels and fine clothes. Rose had thought the Beresford ball impressive, but it paled beside the brilliance of the scene she saw below her.

"The prince will make his entrance shortly," Lady Athena told them as they went through the receiving line. "Rose, please stay close so I might introduce you to His Royal Highness. St. Croix, I believe you have already been presented to the Prince."

"Yes, I have, though I doubt he will remember me. I must congratulate you, Lady Tarasford, on a most impressive setting. It will be the social triumph of the Season, nay, of the next five Seasons, I do assure you."

Lady Tarasford thanked Richard for his compliments, though she frowned slightly at his lazy drawl. "Rose, I must congratulate you on the way you have draped that shawl. I wager it will be the fashion rage after this night."

"Why thank you, Athena. It is very kind of you to say so."

The butler at the top of the stairs signaled the footman at the bottom of the stairs that the royal party was approaching. The footman then whispered the information to Sir Michael, and he, in turn, arranged everyone in the receiving line. He insisted that Rose and Richard stand with them.

The prince and Mrs. Fitzherbert descended the stairs together, her hand on his arm. They were smiling at each other; for all appearances a happy and devoted couple. As they passed down the receiving line, Rose noticed that the prince was very conscientious in including his companion in all introductions and conversations. When the prince reached her, she sank into a deep curtsy.

"Now what have we here? A sweet bud of English

womanhood. Rise, fair maiden, and tell us your name." The prince held out his hand to Rose.

Rose placed her fingers on his and stood. "Rose Maynwaring, if it please Your Royal Highness."

"It pleases us very well. How is it, Miss Maynwaring, we have not had the pleasure of seeing you before this?"

"I have newly come to town, Your Royal Highness."

"Indeed? It gives us great pleasure to have so beautiful a flower grace the room we are in."

"Your Royal Highness, may I present my aunt, Lady Dorington, and my fiancé, Viscount St. Croix." Rose introduced those beside her as etiquette demanded.

"Fiancé? Fortunate man, St. Croix. It will be our pleasure to dance with your lovely lady this evening, if she is willing." The prince turned to Richard.

"We are gratified by your kindness, Your Royal Highness," Richard answered, privately wishing he could spare Rose the difficulties such a dance could bring. The prince was not very light of foot.

Everyone in the room became aware of the conversation going on at the foot of the stairs. For the prince to pay such marked attention to anyone must automatically place the individual high on every hostess's list. Unbeknownst to Rose, her social acceptability immediately became unquestioned. The prince had accepted her, there was no more to be said.

The prince moved on, once again taking Mrs. Fitzherbert's arm. Sir Michael and Lady Tarasford followed in his wake, making introductions and guiding the royal party around the room.

"So, what did you think of Prinny?" Richard asked Rose.

"He is considerably different than I pictured him. Somehow he is more, and less, than I expected."

"How so?"

Rose hesitated for a moment. "More, because he has more presence than what I thought, and less because he seems so very human. Perhaps it is having Mrs. Fitzherbert with him that makes me see a vulnerability."

Richard was pleased with Rose's astute observations. "Yes, he does seem gentler in her presence. Now, shall we dance?"

"Go on, Rose, enjoy yourself. I shall be over with the other dowagers, discussing Mrs. Fitzherbert's gown and Prinny's latest scandal." Lady Dorington gave Rose a little push in Richard's direction.

Richard saw Rose wince with pain when Lady Dorington touched her sore shoulder. "What is it Rose? Are you hurt?" He drew her off to the side of the room.

How can he ask me that? Rose demanded. He knows what happened. He must have seen me fall. She started to reply when they were once again approached by the royal personage. This time only Sir Michael was with him. Lady Tarasford had led Mrs. Fitzherbert over to the punch bowl.

"Ah, there is the young couple. See how they seek each other's company even in a crowded room," the prince said jovially. "But, St. Croix, I hear you are a hero."

"A hero?" Rose turned questioning eyes on Richard.

"What? Didn't you tell your lady? Gads, man, you should have milked it for all it's worth. Your betrothed shot a mad dog in the village today, just as it was about to attack an unwary crofter's child."

The error of her thinking came in a flash to Rose and she blushed with shame that quickly turned to relief. Richard had been in the village helping to rid it of the menace. He couldn't have been the one who shot at her. It must have been a poacher after all!

She felt giddy with relief. It was several moments before she heard what the prince was saying.

"Good man, St. Croix. I say, I do like the cut of that coat. West make it?"

"Of course, Your Royal Highness, who else? If I'm not mistaken, yours is from the same tailor."

The prince nodded happily. "So it is. You can tell a lot about a man from his clothes, St. Croix. A lot about a man."

"Indeed so, Your Royal Highness."

Sir Michael broke into this conversation. "Excuse me, Your Royal Highness, but supper is to be served. Shall we gather up the ladies and proceed?"

"Of course, Tarasford. But I want Miss Maynwaring and Viscount St. Croix seated where we can continue this conversation."

"If I know my Athena, Your Royal Highness, it has already been arranged." Sir Michael led them over to where the ladies waited.

The prince escorted Lady Tarasford in while Sir Michael had Mrs. Fitzherbert on his arm. Richard took in Rose, and the rest of the guests fell in line behind them. Soon they were all seated at the huge banquet table that Lady Tarasford had ornamented with confections made like little Chinese pagodas and temples. Gingerbread men and women, decorated in Oriental dress, lined the street for the procession of a mandarin in his sedan chair.

Rose looked at the elaborate arrangement in amazement. She had never seen anything like it. It must have taken the kitchen staff days to make the tiny figures, all of which would be consumed at the end of the meal.

The repast began, each course presented, approved, served, and removed. Twenty-two in all, Rose counted and wondered how she could possibly eat so much. Or drink so much, she mentally added as a new wine was served with each course. She noticed that Richard would sip sparingly from each goblet, never downing the entire portion as most of the others did, and she followed his example. By the end of the meal, she felt slightly gay, but nowhere near the inebriated state she would have been in if she had drunk all that was served.

Lady Tarasford started to stand and lead the ladies into the drawing room while the men had their cigars and port.

"One moment, Lady Tarasford," the Prince of Wales forestalled her and stood up himself. "We propose a toast. To the newly engaged couple, Miss Rose Maynwaring and Viscount St. Croix."

The toast was made, and the prince continued. "We are most taken with you," he said to Rose and Richard. "And we wish to attend your nuptials. When are they to be held?"

"The second Sunday in March, Your Royal Highness. Your presence would make our wedding remembered by uncountable generations of our descendants."

The prince accepted this compliment as his due and continued. Rose suspected he was inebriated and wished that he would turn his attention elsewhere.

But the prince was shaking his head. "We cannot make it on that date." He paused, as if considering a new idea. "We have it. You shall be married here, tomorrow, in the Tarasfords' chapel. We shall give the bride away and Lady Tarasford shall be matron of honor. Sir Michael can be your best man and all these fine people can be the wedding guests."

A murmur went up from the others seated at the table. The prince took that to mean assent.

"Then it is settled. Tomorrow morning there is to be a wedding." His Royal Highness raised his wineglass again. "To the bride and groom!"

"To the bride and groom," echoed down the table. Rose sat stunned. Where just a few hours before she had planned to end the whole charade, she now found herself in the position of having to marry by royal decree. Richard may not have shot at her, but there were still many things unsettled between them. Now there was no hope of resolving them before the vows were said. The prince did not know what chaos he was causing. Why, she didn't even have a wedding dress! At this thought, her heart wrenched. The beautiful gown that Madame Vereaux had designed would go for naught. Instead of the stately ceremony she had envisaged, her wedding would be a slipshod affair thrown together for a royal whim!

Chapter Seven

IT WAS A bleary-eyed Rose that hazily watched Tillie open the drapes of her room.

"Sleep well, miss?" the maid asked cheerily.

Rose just flopped back on the pillows and closed her eyes against the light. It had been a rotten night, filled with half dreams and little rest. Slowly she realized there was an awful lot of light streaming from the window to be early morning. "What time is it?" she asked Tillie, raising one eyelid.

"Near on to noon, miss. Lady Tarasford and the viscount said what I should let you sleep in on account of this being your wedding day and all."

"My wedding day!" Rose bolted up in the bed. Full realization of what this day meant hit her suddenly.

Tillie came to stand beside the bed, her hands folded primly in front of her apron. "I would like to say, on behalf of the staff, that we wish you all the happiness in the world, miss."

Rose looked balefully at the maid. "Thank you, Tillie, and thank the staff for me. I truly regret causing them to alter their normal Sunday routine."

"Oh, miss, t'ain't a thing to worry about. Cook, he's having the time of his life and the gardener is so pleased to show what he can produce even if it is

February he's bustin' buttons. Don't you worry none. We'll do you proud."

"The one I feel sorry for is Lady Tarasford. Her beautiful house party turned all topsy-turvy because of this."

"Did I hear my name mentioned?" Tillie was just admitting Lady Tarasford. "Don't you worry about me, Rose. This wedding will make my little weekend gathering the talk of at least five Seasons to come. But I wanted to show you what just arrived from London." She gestured to the stack of boxes Tillie was taking from a footman.

Rose recognized the white-and-mauve boxes of Madame Vereaux's shop. When Lady Tarasford opened the largest and withdrew a wedding gown, Rose gave a little exclamation. "How in the world did these get here?"

"They came by post, miss. 'Coo, that's the prettiest gown I've ever seen." Tillie took the dress carefully from Lady Tarasford and gathered up the long train of the skirt. "I'll take it and press it right away. It'll be ready for you by the time you have finished your bath, miss."

"Thank you, Lady Tarasford, for going to such trouble. Though how you managed to get Madame Vereaux to finish it so quickly, I have no idea."

"Oh, my dear, it wasn't me. Richard had his man go to London." Lady Tarasford began to untie the ribbons on the other boxes. "I imagine he had to pay quite an exorbitant price to have these things ready and sent here. I had no idea he was so thoughtful. You are a very good influence on him, Rose. Who would have thought a man could be so sensitive to a woman's needs." She nodded her head in approval at the boxes on the bed. "Almost all of your trousseau is here. Of course, you will want to add to it in Paris."

Paris! Rose suddenly remembered that they would be embarking on that journey this very afternoon, right after dinner. Richard had seemed particularly determined that they leave Tarasford Hall as soon as decency would permit. Why was he in such a hurry? Could it be he wished to be alone with her to carry out the threats he made in the gallery? Did he need to possess her so much that he could not wait a day?

"I'll have Rachel come and do your hair," Athena continued. "Tillie is coming along quite nicely, but today requires a more experienced dresser, I think." Lady Tarasford went to the door.

"Thank you, Athena. It is very kind of you," Rose said as the lady of the house exited.

Meanwhile, Richard was being visited by Sir Michael, who set Gillis at the door of Richard's room to guard against unwanted listeners.

"Everything is in readiness, boy." The older man positioned himself at the small desk. "Your yacht awaits you at Hastings to take you across the Channel with the morning tide and with all the appropriate ceremony. Your first contact will be at the Sangre de Roi in Beauvais. It's a gambling hall, so no one will comment on the rakehell St. Croix paying it a visit during his stopover. There you will meet with Pierre Rouen, who will pass on the arrangements made for contacting the others."

"Sangre de Roi, Beauvais." Richard memorized the location. "I've met Rouen, so there's no problem there." He took up his waistcoat and slipped his arms into it. "Do you think Fitzsimmons is properly convinced of my evil ways?"

"Have no doubt about it. It galls me that a man of his status should be an informant for Bonaparte." Sir Michael slapped his palm down on the desktop in agitation. "What kind of power does that Frenchman have that he can draw so many English away from their true loyalties?"

"Shall I ask him when I see him?" Richard drew himself into the haughty stance he had adopted for his new role. "My dear little colonel, would you mind awfully telling me how you corrupt everything you come in contact with?"

"Watch yourself, St. Croix. Bonaparte is no fool. Already he is setting up situations to make us look bad in the eyes of the world. He claims that our seizure of French ships in the Channel is unlawful and against the Treaty of Amiens. We know he is massing troops in a new location, though we do not yet know precisely where. There are also rumors of a massive navy being built. I want you to find out more about these things, and any other information you can glean, and get it back to us as soon as possible."

"That is my intention, sir. And, then, I suppose I shall retire from this life and turn to managing my estates, or raising cows, or some such thing." There was a real note of regret in Richard's voice.

"How so, lad? Are you tired of the adventurer's life?"

"Never. But I am soon to be a married man, Sir Michael. I can hardly expect Rose to tolerate a husband who disappears for unaccountable times and takes on an entire pantheon of personalities. No, I fear this is my last adventure, sir."

"I wonder, my boy," Sir Michael half mumbled to himself. "Still, this is your wedding day and we should be celebrating. His Royal Highness is preparing in his own chambers. Be ready for anything Prinny may do. I should keep myself between your bride and the prince, if I were you."

"To be sure, Sir Michael. We are leaving right after the wedding feast. I plan to spend the night at the King's Arms in Hastings and sail on the morning tide. That will put us into Dieppe in good time to make Beauvais before dark."

"Lord Admiral Fitzsimmons, sir," Gillis said, opening the door to admit the elderly man.

Richard instantly fell completely into his St. Croix role. "Gadzooks, Admiral, what a kind consideration. Coming to commiserate with the condemned man."

"Nonsense, St. Croix," the admiral frowned heavily at him. "It is the duty of every man to marry and produce an heir. And, from what I've seen of your bride, that shouldn't be too onerous a task." He chortled heavily into his own mustache.

Richard resisted the urge to cram the ends of the man's mustache down his throat. Fitzsimmons had just recently been revealed as a French informant and the Depot had decided to manipulate him for its own ends. Before his exposure, he had managed to send incredibly damaging information to Paris about the British ship movements. Eventually he would hang, Richard knew, but not until the Depot had wrung every last use it could from him.

"As you say, sir, 'tis my duty." Richard signaled for Gillis to come and tie his cravat. "What do you think, gentlemen? Do I present the appropriate image of the happy bridegroom?"

"Indeed, St. Croix, the epitome of fashion," Sir Michael acknowledged.

"Would anyone care to wager on the amount of wine consumed at my wedding feast?" Richard addressed them both blandly. "Or, perhaps a small bet on how long it will be before my bride conceives our first offspring?"

Lord Admiral Fitzsimmons frowned heavily at him. "Really, sir, I do not believe this is an appropriate time for such thoughts."

Richard spread his hands outward as if in apology. "Perhaps you are right. How about a wager on the first child being a male?"

The admiral merely snorted.

Rose stood in the vestibule of the little chapel in the Norman wing of Tarasford Hall. Beside her, the Prince of Wales was taking his place to lead her down the aisle. Lady Tarasford would precede them, acting as the matron of honor. She smoothed the convent lace of the tight-fitting bodice, lightly fingering the white silk georgette that covered the pale blue underdress. Married in blue, your love will be true, she thought sardonically.

"Ready, my dear?" Lady Tarasford pulled back from where she had peeked through the concealing curtains. "The vicar, Sir Michael, and Richard have all taken their places."

"I would like to take this moment to thank you, Your Royal Highness, for your kindness in participating in my wedding." Rose tried to keep the anxiety she felt out of her voice.

"It is our pleasure, my dear. Our pleasure." He repeated himself as he took her arm. He had adopted his fatherly pose for the day, a fact Rose was most thankful for.

Tillie gave Rose's train one more twitch. "So's everyone can see the pretty cutout lace flowers," she explained. And then she held back the curtain for Lady Tarasford, the prince, and Rose to step through.

The chapel was filled with the houseguests. Rose kept her eyes riveted on the altar at the front and the man who waited for her there.

Richard stood tall and incredibly handsome beside Sir Michael and the vicar. He turned to watch her coming down the aisle and his eyes lit up. She was a vision only possible in the dreams of a hopeless romantic. Her dark hair, freed from its pins, fell in sable splendor down her back and was crowned by a wreath of white-and-pink roses and blue forget-me-nots. The gown that had caused him so much trouble to get from London flowed around Rose's trim form like gossamer waves of pale blue and white. A feeling of possession rose up in him. This incredible creature was now his!

Rose saw Richard's searing look and blushed. Her hand trembled on the prince's arm and when it was placed in Richard's, her heart fluttered in anticipation and fear. From some distant place she heard Richard's voice promising to love, honor, and cherish her, and then her own voice repeating the vows that would bind her to him for life. The weight of the gold band he slid on her finger seemed disproportionate to the size of the ring, and suddenly it was done. Richard drew her to him and kissed her before the assemblage.

Once again she fell into the maelstrom of emotion his kiss caused in her, but this time, before she was completely lost, he pulled away. Rose leaned slightly into him, needing support, and placed her hand lightly on his chest.

"Easy love," he whispered, covering her hand with his. "It's time to face the masses." He gently turned her around to face the guests and led her back down the aisle and out the front of the chapel.

A few moments later they were joined by the prince, the Tarasfords, and Mrs. Fitzherbert. The group hurried down the connecting corridor into the Italian dining room and organized themselves into the receiving line. It wasn't long before the guests arrived and Rose was occupied by the demands of good etiquette.

She smiled, was bussed by the males, hugged by the females, and tolerated risqué double entendres for over half an hour. Finally Lady Tarasford called a halt and asked the prince to lead the way to the wedding feast.

Richard slipped her arm through his and guided her to her place of honor. After seating Rose, he sat down to her left, the prince on her right. Mrs. Fitzherbert ended up on Richard's left. Leaning forward, Rose could see Lady Dorington seated with Sir Michael.

With great dignity, the butler announced the meal and the guests watched as platter after platter was paraded around by liveried footmen.

"How wonderfully medieval," one female guest commented and clapped in delight when the dessert, a huge *gateau* of sponge cake, chocolate and cream, was carried in by four servants and placed on the table in the center of the U-shaped arrangements.

"Athena, how could your cook contrive so much in such a short time!" Rose exclaimed, amazed by the bounty before them.

"I must agree, Lady Tarasford," the prince said, happily perusing the dressed salmon placed in front of him. "This is fare worthy of Carlton House."

"My staff will be so pleased to hear that, Your Royal Highness," Lady Tarasford acknowledged the compliment.

Despite the sumptuous dishes, Rose found she had no desire to eat. Though she managed to appear gay, deep inside her, her stomach knotted in a hard lump and her hands and knees felt shaky. She could neither forget that she was now tied to this man who sat beside her, nor the conversation in the gallery. What would this night bring? What did she want it to bring? Part of her was undeniably drawn to Richard. Was this how her mother had felt? Was she, like her mother, unable to control those baser passions that no woman who was truly a lady was supposed to feel? She studied Richard through lowered lashes. What was going through his mind?

Rose would have been surprised to find how closely Richard's thoughts paralleled her own, with one notable exception. He couldn't wait to get out of this menagerie and on the road for Hastings. He had noticed Rose's want of appetite and put it down to maidenly nervousness. She looked so fetching, how could he, now that she was his, keep his hands off her? Surely he must be some kind of throwback to his Celtic ancestry to so strongly desire to carry her off. He feared that once he had bedded her, it would be addictive and any chance to maintain his sanguine facade in regard to Rose would be gone. He had best make up his mind here and now to restrain himself until after the mission.

The butler approached the bride and groom with a huge silver knife decorated with white heather.

"Rose, Richard, would you please cut the first slice from the cake?" Lady Tarasford invited them to do the honors. "You must feed the first slice to your new husband, my dear, as a sign of your obedience."

A sudden rebellion flared up in Rose. I'd like to ram it down his throat! she thought as she took the knife and allowed Richard to escort her to the cake. They performed the little ceremony to the cheers of all present. Rose turned the knife back over to the butler and returned to her seat, followed by Richard.

"Your attention, ladies and gentlemen, His Royal Highness, the Prince of Wales, would like to propose a toast," the butler announced in stentorian tones.

The prince rose and raised his wineglass. "To the new Viscount and Viscountess St. Croix. May their union be long and fruitful." He downed the goblet's contents in one swallow.

The other guests raised their own and followed suit.

"It has come to our attention that we have yet to bestow a wedding gift on this fine couple," the prince continued.

Rose began to suspect that the prince was somewhat the worse for the wine he had imbibed. To her surprise, he pulled off two of the diamond-and-ruby buttons on his waistcoat and presented them to her with a flourish.

"My dear, we wish to make amends for that oversight. Make some ear bobs from them." He pressed them into her hand. "And for you, St. Croix, we give you this." The prince removed one of his three watch fobs and handed it to Richard.

"I, ah, am overwhelmed, Your Royal Highness," Richard said.

"Indeed, I shall cherish these always." Rose smiled at the tipsy prince.

More toasts were proposed and drunk, until Lady Tarasford finally stood up to lead the women from the room. "We shall escort Rose to her room to change. I know you are anxious to be on your way, my dears."

As she climbed the steps, Rose found Mrs. Fitzherbert by her side. The woman smiled gently at her. "Don't worry my dear. I shall see you get something more practical. A tea service, I think. His Royal Highness is very impulsive, but we women know that it takes more than buttons to run a household."

Rose was so surprised, it took a moment for her to respond. "That is very kind of you, Mrs. Fitzherbert, but I do assure you I am overwhelmed by His Royal Highness's generosity."

"Of course you are." The older woman patted her hand. "Still, one can always use a tea service. It shall be my gift, in appreciation for providing this delightfully romantic weekend."

All Rose could do was thank her.

Once Rose had reached her chamber door, the other women left her to position themselves below. Only Aunt Bernie and Lady Tarasford stayed behind. Tillie opened the door for them.

"Oh, my lady, it was so beautiful!" the little maid exclaimed.

It took Rose a moment to realize Tillie was speaking to her. It was the first time anyone had addressed her in accordance with her new title.

"My lady, your traveling clothes are all laid out. Would you care to change?"

"I suppose I should." Rose gently lifted the wreath of flowers from her head. Lady Tarasford took them from her, along with her bouquet. She drew a few of the blossoms from each and made a small corsage to pin to Rose's cloak. "You can press these in your Bible."

"Thank you, Athena."

As she dressed, Rose couldn't help but notice how quiet her aunt had become. "Aunt Bernie, I shall be fine, truly. After all, I'm the Viscountess St. Croix now."

"As if you cared a fig for that! No, my dear, it is the other aspects of marriage I am concerned about. I would not see you misused."

"Aunt Bernie, if you are referring to the more physical duty of a wife, rest assured I am prepared." But am I? she wondered even as she said the words.

"Really, Bernie, I know Richard will have every care of Rose. And, frankly speaking, there is nothing quite like the physical expression of a man's love to make a woman feel completely content," Lady Tarasford commented with a wicked little smile. "Of course, it is quite shocking of me to say so, but we are all married women here now."

All this time Tillie had been folding away Rose's wedding finery into the traveling trunks, but from the turn of the maid's head and the slowness she went about the task, Rose could tell she was listening to every word.

"Not everyone here is a married woman," Rose said, nodding toward Tillie.

Seeing herself the object of her employer's interest, Tillie blushed a deep red. "Oh, my lady, 'tis nothing I haven't heard before. I come from a large family."

"Of course she has. It's part of being in service." Lady Dorington rose and crossed to her niece. "I shall go below now. There will be little chance there to say our farewells, so I shall do it here. Remember, Rose, your room at Swallows' Walk will always be waiting for you, should you wish to return for any reason."

She still isn't certain about Richard, Rose thought. "Thank you, Aunt, I shall remember that." She finished buttoning the spenser of her periwinkle traveling ensemble.

Tillie handed her the matching bouquet. "My lady, his lordship says that, if you will have me, I might attend you on your wedding trip. My bundle's already and I can leave as soon as you give your permission. If'n such arrangements are agreeable to you, my lady."

"They are most agreeable. But, are you certain you want to leave your family and friends?" Rose accepted the hat but paused before putting it on.

"It'll be an adventure. And, maybe, if everything suits your ladyship, it might become a permanent position." The maid's voice was a curious mixture of hesitation and self-assurance.

"I think that very likely. It shall be very pleasant to have you along, Tillie."

"Oh, thank you, my lady!" The maid bobbed a curtsy.

"You'd best see to getting these trunks loaded. When the viscount sets his mind to a schedule, he doesn't like to be delayed."

"Oh, yes, my lady!" Tillie hurried off to summon the footmen to take the last of the luggage to the waiting carriages.

"And, now," Rose said, "I suppose, it is time to go down." Rose took up her gloves and began drawing them on.

"We shall precede you and let Richard know you are coming. They are all in the vestibule, drinking champagne toasts." Lady Tarasford gave Rose a little hug. "All the best, my dear."

Aunt Bernie, too, drew her arms around Rose. "Every happiness, my gel. And remember, Swallows' Walk awaits."

Rose felt tears build hotly behind her eyes. "Thank you, thank you both." She swallowed hard as she saw the two women exit. Well, Rose, she addressed herself in an attempt to buck up her courage. It is time to go forward and face the enemy. She lingered on that thought. Was Richard her enemy? Why had she thought of that peculiar phrase? She was about to embark to a strange land, inhabited by people who were her traditional adversaries, with only a tenuous relationship with a man who now had full, legal control over her. Was it any wonder she felt some anxiety?

Richard saw Rose come across the gallery and start down the final flight of steps. He rushed up them, two at a time, to meet her. "Ready, my dear, to quit these noisy premises?"

Rose hesitated. She'd be alone with him once they went through that door and entered the waiting carriage. "As you wish, my lord. But, perhaps, we should have one last glass of champagne with our hosts."

Richard looked deeply into Rose's eyes and read the uncertainty there. "Of course." He escorted her to the bottom of the steps and guided her to where the Tarasfords, the Prince of Wales and Mrs. Fitzherbert, and Lady Dorington were standing. A footman offered them refreshments and Richard raised his glass high. A hush settled on the crowd as the others realized that the groom was about to propose a toast.

"Your Royal Highness, Lady Tarasford, Mrs. Fitzherbert, Sir Michael, friends. You know I am a gambling man. I would like to propose a wager." His words brought snickers and a few derisive comments. "I wager," Richard commented, "that nowhere in the world could kindness and generosity of our hosts be matched. I propose a toast to Sir Michael and Lady Athena Tarasford."

Amid the "here, heres" the wine was drunk. Richard took Rose's glass and set it on a nearby salver. "And now, we must be going if we are going to reach Hastings by dark. Come, my love, the carriage is waiting."

The prince escorted them to the conveyance himself and graciously handed Rose up. Without looking to see who had caught it, Rose tossed the wedding bouquet and ducked inside. Richard quickly followed and fell into the seat next to her. A groom adjusted the warmed bricks and fox-lap throw for them and then closed the carriage door. Finally the coach lurched forward and they were on their way.

"Gads, what a show!" Richard exclaimed as he leaned back against the squabs. "Far more wearying than a whole night at Boodles. You must be fagged to death."

"Not at all, my lord. Though I am relieved to get away from the royal personage. I felt rather constrained in his presence." Rose tucked the lap robe tighter around her legs, thus creating a definite line between their two bodies.

"I understand what you mean. Prinny can be difficult, though I must say, he was very well behaved on this occasion. I half expected him to invoke the old right of 'first night.' " Richard gave her a possessive grin.

Rose didn't rise to his bait. "Indeed? Is that why you were in such a hurry to leave, my lord?"

"What is this formality?" Richard asked irritably. "Richard. You agreed to call me Richard. Remember?"

"A wife must obey her husband's commands, Richard." Rose tried unsuccessfully to suppress a mischievous smile.

Seeing it, Richard relaxed and put his arm around her shoulders. "And don't you forget it." He pulled her into the crook of his shoulder. "We shall get on well, Rose. I promise you that." His voice took on a serious note. "All I ask is that you reserve judgment until you learn all the facts. Do not formulate your opinion of me based on rumors and innuendos you may hear."

Is he referring to his association to Mrs. Wessex? Rose wondered. Or is he warning me? She pulled back a bit so she could see his finely chiseled features. "Alas, I am hardly one to cast stones. After all, my reputation has its own stains."

"How so?"

"The nature of my birth. My mother's, ah, conduct. Society looks for these flaws in me."

Not liking the distance she had put between them, Richard gently pulled her back against his side. "You put too much emphasis on the past, Rose. We have a future now, together." He lifted Rose's chin and gently kissed her lips.

Rose felt herself succumbing to the gentle persuasion of his lips. Why not? she asked herself. He is my husband now. It is my duty, she warmed to his touch, my most pleasurable duty to submit to his embraces. All coherent thought dissolved beneath the delicious sweetness of the kiss.

When they broke, it was Richard's turn to withdraw a bit. Steady man, he reminded himself, You're supposed to be keeping her at arm's length. Another embrace like that one and there will be a little Stanton before Christmas.

"Oh, look, Richard. The villagers have come out to see us pass."

Richard looked out the carriage window and saw it was true. They were rumbling through the main street of the little hamlet and it seemed that the place's entire population had come out to wave and wish them well. "This is ridiculous," Richard protested, embarrassed. "All I did was shoot a dog."

Cries of "Long live the viscount and his bride," "Many blessings on your house," and "Many wee ones," greeted them as they reached the small well in the center of town.

"We should stop, Richard. Just for a moment."

"Oh, very well." Richard reached up and tapped on the roof of the carriage to get the driver's attention.

The horses were pulled to a stop and a groom hopped off the back to open the door for the viscount. Richard stood in the opening and waved to the crowd. "The viscountess and I are overwhelmed by this display of well-wishing. Thank you all for this, ah, warm demonstration."

A small girl with a handful of flowers was pushed forward. "These be fer yer missus," she lisped and held up the stems.

"Rose, you have a visitor," Richard whispered back into the coach and stepped out of the doorway to allow Rose to appear.

When Rose emerged, a new set of cheers went up. For a lady of her stature to be so gracious as to actually let the villagers see her, that was quality indeed!

Rose leaned down and accepted the flowers, pressing a silver piece into the child's hand. "Thank you, my dear. They are lovely. You save that coin for your own dowry. And someday you will be as fortunate as I have been."

Overwhelmed, the child just stared at her with huge, watery blue eyes.

From the door of the hamlet's one alehouse, another figure watched the proceedings at the well. He half turned to the others crowded around him. "Just another 'igh-n-mighty."

"Not 'im, guv. 'E killed a mad dog fer us. I 'ear 'e's all right, as such goes."

"Me pretty, Annie, she works up at the 'all. Says their 'eaded fer 'astings. Strange place fer a weddin' night, if'n ye ask me." One of the tavern boys threw in. "Me, I'd find me the closest mattress an' that would be that."

"G'arn, ye don't even know which end to tiddle, Barney," the older men scoffed.

" 'Astings ye say? Got friends there I spose. More o' 'em what's feeds on the sweat o' the rest o' us." The stranger spat.

Barney, not to be intimidated by his elders, tried to increase his importance as a source of information. "Naw. They be stayin' at a' inn. The King's Arms no less."

The stranger merely harrumphed as if that proved his low opinion of the titled classes. Privately he thought, "The King's Arms is it. If'n I cut across the countryside, I kin reach 'Astings afore 'em an' set a bit o' a surprise fer the 'aughty viscount. A surprise what will net me a pretty penny." He didn't wait to see the coach move on, but headed straight for his horse.

Chapter Eight

THE CARRIAGE RUMBLED on, followed by the second coach with Tillie, Gillis, and all the luggage. When the coach made its first post stop, Richard helped Rose out of the coach to stretch her legs while new bricks were brought to replace the now cool ones.

Watching her perambulate around the inn yard, Richard was struck with an overwhelming desire to be totally alone with his new bride, without maids, nosy innkeepers, even Gillis. Why shouldn't they have this one night together? he reasoned. His yacht was at the dock in Hastings. They could spend the night on board rather than at the King's Arms. True, it would be easier to keep his earlier resolve in the environs of the crowded hostelry, but he convinced himself he had enough willpower to enjoy an evening alone with Rose without it leading to more physical developments. Richard summoned Gillis and explained the change in plans.

"You and Tillie go ahead to the King's Arms and let them know I've changed my plans. You can join us aboard ship in the morning."

Gillis flashed his gold tooth. "As you say, my lord. The ship has been supplied, so you won't want for anything." The older man waved for the driver and postboys to mount up. "I'll see you in the morning, my lord," he said with a wicked wink in Richard's direction.

A muffled figure stood in the dark shadows created by the torches that lit the inn yard, his shoulder leaning against the stable wall. The high collar of his cape hid the tight-lipped smile of satisfaction he made when he saw the Viscount St. Croix's advance coach pull in. It would now only be a matter of making up to one of the serving wenches to find out the viscount's rooms and his job would be wrapped up nice and tight. He slid a small, blue, glass bottle from the pocket of his cloak and hefted it slightly in his half-mittened hand. A few drops of this and the high and mighty viscount and his bride would never wake from their wedding night.

He watched as the passengers from the advance coach disembarked. The first out was the viscount's valet, followed by a girl who looked as if she were about to pass out at any minute.

"Proprietor!" Gillis, alias Hamstead, bellowed, taking Tillie's arm to support her.

The girl gave a little start at the loudness of his voice and grimaced in pain.

The innkeeper came rushing over. Taking in the girl's condition, he quickly assisted them to the door.

As they walked forward, Gillis explained that the viscount would not be stopping at the King's Arms after all. He softened the proprietor's disappointment with a coin pouch, thus insuring the good treatment of himself and Tillie. "The viscount will be spending the night on his yacht, the *Cassiopea*."

"I do 'ope 'is lordship will 'onor us another time," the owner said, accepting the pouch.

"That will depend on my report on your establishment, innkeep," Gillis informed him haughtily. "Now, please assist the viscountess's maid to her room and provide her with some sop. The girl got dreadfully ill in the coach. Heaven help us if she's like this the entire way to France!" Gillis spun his head around as he heard a muffled curse coming from the shadows behind him. "What's that? Who's there?"

But when he looked, there was no one. The lurker had managed to slip into the stable.

With yet another curse, the would-be assassin stomped to his horse, hidden behind the building, and mounted. His employer was sure to be displeased with this turn of events and that meant no money pouch and a cuff on the ear besides if he didn't figure a way to turn matters around. Pausing, he thought back over Gillis's words. The boat wouldn't be that hard to locate if it was tied up to the quay. There was still a chance he'd be able to complete his mission and get his money from Mr. Timothy Ralston. That dandy, he knew, was even now in London, ready to express his grief over the loss of his cousins and to make certain all knew he had been in town when the tragedy occurred. The assassin wheeled his horse and headed for the wharf.

"Richard, this hardly looks like an inn." Rose pulled her head back from the carriage window and regarded her husband. She had seen the high masts and bowsprits silhouetted against the late twilight sky.

Richard took a deep breath. He had tried to bring himself to tell Rose of his change in plans several times, but the words just weren't there. Finally he had decided to just let it happen and hope she wouldn't kick up a fuss. "I thought we'd spend the night on the *Cassiopea*."

Rose waited for him to go on and explain the change in plans. When he didn't, she eyed him suspiciously. "I don't see Hamstead or Tillie, or even the coach they were in. Were they so far ahead of us that they are all unloaded and cozy aboard your boat?"

"Ship. The *Cassiopea* is a ship. A sloop actually. Small, I grant you, for the class, but a yacht hardly needs to be as large as a ship of the line. I sailed on her a couple of times before my cousin passed away." He continued to talk such roundaboutations as he helped her out of the carriage and led her toward the gangplank.

"You still haven't told me where Tillie and your man are." She allowed him to slip her arm through his as they walked. What game was he playing now? she wondered as they approached the narrow plank of wood that spanned the water between the pier and the ship's deck.

A distinguished, older man, his face bewhiskered with muttonchops that ran into an iron gray mustache of noble proportions came across the little bridge. "My lord, we were not expecting you."

"My dear, allow me to present Captain Deering." Richard introduced Rose to the senior officer. "We've decided to spend the night on board, Captain. I trust you will not be incommoded."

"Not at all, sir. The *Cassiopea* is, after all, your ship. I was planning to spend the evening onshore, but, now that you have arrived . . ." he was cut short by Richard.

"Nonsense, Captain Deering. Continue with your plans. Frankly, my wife and I will enjoy the privacy."

The captain chuckled. "I see. Please, allow me to escort you to your cabin. Everything is in readiness there for you. With your permission, I will precede the viscountess so I might help her on the other side of the plank. There is only the watch aboard, two good men, but hardly gentlemen." Seeing the viscount's nod, he retraced his steps.

Rose scrambled nimbly over the plank and stepped down onto the deck of the ship. She tried to sort out her thoughts as they waited for Richard. It was patently obvious that Richard had contrived for them to be alone this evening. To what end? Was he planning on establishing a more intimate relationship with her? All the doubts that had plagued her since that morning rose up again to make her heart palpitate with anxiety.

The captain led them to the sheltered gangway that led down into the aft third of the ship. Since the *Cassiopea* was a pleasure yacht, more space had been allocated for cabins and amenities than any cargo ship could afford. There was a central area with five doors leading from it. Captain Deering led them to the one centered on the farthest wall and held it open for them. "Your cabin, Viscount St. Croix. I shall have a crewman deliver a repast for you and your lady if you wish."

"Do that, Captain. And have a pleasant time ashore. We shall see you in the morning."

Rose entered the cabin and looked around in surprise. Everything was pleasantly efficient without too much feeling of cramped space. She studiously tried to keep her eyes from the bunk, which seemed to dominate the room from its location against the left wall. A window cut into the back of the ship was covered with small lead panes similar to those set in Swallows' Walk during the time of Elizabeth. She crossed over to peer out at the stygian water below.

"Why so pensive, my love?" Richard moved to stand behind her.

Rose could feel the warmth of his breath on the back of her neck as he spoke. It sent a curious tingle down her spine and she felt strangely vulnerable. When Richard slipped an arm about her shoulders, her knees began to quiver. She gently pulled away, not wanting him to know how his physical presence was affecting her. " 'Tis nothing, Richard. I am merely weary from the day."

Richard allowed her to retreat to the small desk built into the side of the cabin. "And no wonder. First Prinny, then the coach drive. I feel a bit fagged myself. What say we have a bit to eat and go right to bed?"

Rose turned huge eyes on him. "Bed?"

Richard couldn't resist teasing his bride more. He had already resolved to sleep on the window seat, uncomfortable though that may be. It was the penance he must do for having gotten himself in this ridiculous situation. "That is where one usually sleeps," he hesitated, timing his next comment, "as well as other pleasurable pursuits, is it not?"

Rose had no idea what to say to that. She looked around the cabin hoping to find something to distract Richard's thoughts away from the trend they were taking. Her eyes lighted on a small chess set on the desk. "While we're waiting, would you care for a game?"

Amused, Richard nodded.

Rose moved the chess set to the only other furniture in the room, a small table with two chairs. She arranged the pieces, then took the two queens and hid them behind her back. "You choose."

She looks almost like a little girl with her hands behind her back that way, Richard thought. He indicated her right hand. Rose revealed the white queen, which allowed Richard to make the first move.

Using the shadows of the night, the killer skulked aboard the deck of the *Cassiopea*, ducking behind the water barrels that were lashed to the deck. He saw the watch at each end of the ship and pulled back further into concealment. How was he to get to the viscount and viscountess? No doubt they were in one of the cabins below. He disliked frontal attacks—there was too much chance of being killed himself.

He much preferred poisons or "accidents." All this could have been avoided if those two sailors hadn't thwarted his efforts on the Guildford Road. As he was thinking, he heard footsteps coming up the gangplank.

" 'Tis me, Charlie. I brought the vittals fer our passengers," a youthful voice called out to the watch.

"Wait there till I can see ye," one of the watch replied.

The cabin boy placed the heavy tray on top of the lashed water barrels and obediently waited until the watch came close enough with his lantern to see his face. He wasn't aware of the hand that slipped under the cover of the tray.

Grinning at his good fortune, the assassin put several drops from his bottle into the apple dumplings. The image of Rose and Richard biting into the delicious-smelling dessert pleased him immensely. They'd begin to feel sleepy and go to bed, expecting to be in France in the morning. But they'd never make the crossing now. All he had to do was wait until the boy went below and the watch went back to the bow of the ship and he'd be gone.

The cabin boy took up the tray and headed for the cabins below. The watch, however, chose to position himself by one gangplank, preventing the assassin's escape. The brigand pulled himself into a tight ball behind the barrels to wait it out.

Richard held one of the chairs for her, then seated himself. He opened by moving his queen's red pawn.

Rose started by opening the way for her black knight. She sat back and waited for Richard's next move.

The game progressed smoothly, neither side winning an advantage. Richard became impressed with Rose's method of play. She was daring and imaginative, and he realized only his greater experience was keeping him one move ahead of her. She had maneuvered his queen into jeopardy when the meal arrived.

"Shall we postpone the conclusion of this until after we've eaten?" Richard suggested as he took the tray from the sailor.

"Ah ha! You just want to distract me to throw my game off. Your queen is in peril. This should not take long to conclude." Rose, excited about the possibility of winning, waved the tray aside.

"Very well, my dear. As you say, it should not take long." He reseated himself and, instead of moving his queen, he relocated his knight.

Frowning, Rose took his queen. Why had he ignored the queen's obvious danger?

Richard moved his rook. "And that, my dear, is checkmate. Now, shall we dine?"

Rose berated herself for falling for such an obvious trick. He had diverted her attention with a flamboyant play of his queen while he slyly slipped the two lesser pieces in to checkmate her king. "I suppose we may as well." She began to clear the table of the game.

Where the sailor had gotten the food, neither of them had any idea or cared. There were chicken breasts basted in wine, scallops, and apple dumplings. Not as luxurious as the feast they had partaken earlier, but very good nonetheless.

"I think that the seafarers of Hastings have been keeping a secret from the rest of England," Richard commented as he finished up his scallops.

Rose, who hadn't eaten much at the feast, suddenly realized she was very hungry, and thirsty. Richard politely filled her wineglass as she emptied it and she smiled appreciatively at him. Unfortunately there was nothing else to drink in the room. The wine gradually made her relax, and the cabin became very warm.

"I think, my pet, it is time to put you to bed." Richard rose from the table and came around to help her up.

"I can't go to bed," Rose objected. "Tillie isn't here to undo my buttons." She realized that she was slightly inebriated and blushed.

"I'll undo your buttons. Turn around." Richard waited patiently while Rose turned her back on him. He carefully undid each of the little, fabric-covered balls, feeling clumsy beside the daintiness of her form. Once he had finished, he stood back. "I'm going up on deck for a smoke while you finish."

Rose watched him duck out of the door in bewilderment that quickly turned to amusement. Could Richard be too embarrassed to watch her undress? Who would have thought it? Did he run out of the room when Amelia Wessex disrobed? Maybe she wasn't doing it right. Was there some secret to taking your clothes off before a man to make yourself alluring? Rose realized it was the wine making her mind follow these peculiar thoughts, but she continued to dwell on them.

How would Amelia Wessex take off her clothes? she wondered and then remembered a particularly colorful passage in a French novel she had read in her adolescence. In it, the wanton woman had slowly slipped her chemise from her shoulders. Rose tried this maneuver, but with no mirror, it was difficult to see the effect. There had been something about sensually rolling down some silk stockings, too, so Rose tried that only to find she would have to take off her shoes first. Even then, she needed to sit on the edge of the bed to get her hose off. Now what? Rose looked around for a nightdress and realized with a giggle that none of her bags were there. She didn't even have a nightcap. What was she going to wear to bed?

Her eyes fell on the discarded chemise. If she wore that and one of her petticoats, it would make a nightdress of sorts. Anyway, it would have to do. She pulled the fine linen top back on and retied the pink ribbon that kept it closed in front.

The wine began to make her feel woozy. She laid back on the bed to let the dizziness pass and promptly fell asleep.

A dark figure launched itself from some barrels near the gangplank. Richard threw his arm up to protect himself from the dagger he saw held in the assailant's hand. The attacker fell full force against him and Richard was pushed back against the rail.

" 'Ere, what's that. 'Ho's there?" The watch called out as they came running from opposite ends of the ship.

Richard was struggling with the man with the knife. He couldn't see the killer's features in the little light given from the moon and watch lamps. Again the killer tried to stab him with the blade. Richard captured the descending blade by grabbing the man's wrist with both his hands. He twisted, intending to bang the wrist against the railing, but his movement caused the attacker to be off balance and he went over the side with a splash.

Richard leaned over the rail and caught a glimpse of the assassin swimming away. Grim-faced, he turned to the two on watch. "How did he get on board?"

The two sailors tried to make excuses, but Richard waved them away. Whoever it had been, he had known his business. If his own reflexes hadn't been so quick, he'd have been dead by now from a slit throat. But who could be behind such an attack? Had someone learned the real purpose of his trip to France? Was this one of Bonaparte's hired assassins? But how? The men of the Military Depot were a small, highly select group. Who could be an informer?

Lost in thought, Richard made his way down the companionway to the cabin. He smiled slightly as he saw the dinner tray, complete with untouched dessert, set out by the door.

Upon entering, he found Rose curled up on the bed, sound asleep. Smiling softly, he brushed a strand of hair back from her eyes and drew the coverlet over her body. "Sweet dreams, my love," he said and gently kissed her forehead.

Sighing, he took the spare blanket from the foot of the bed and a pillow and went to the window seat. After drawing off his boots and removing all except his shirt and breeches, he tried to accommodate his six-foot-two frame on its hard surface. He lay with his head cushioned on the palm of his hand and contemplated Rose's form in the bed. She was such a slight little thing, she hardly took up any room in it at all. She was sound asleep so it would make no difference to her if he abjured the hard window seat for the comfort of a mattress. If he turned his back to her, he could pretend he was back in his military days sleeping with his men for warmth.

With these resolves, he took up the pillow and blanket once again and moved to the bed. Gently lifting the covers so as not to disturb Rose, he slipped into the cool sheets. The lilac scent of Rose's perfume wafted about him and he knew there was no way he could pretend she wasn't there. It was going to be a long, difficult night.

The light touch of Richard's lips had brought Rose out of her slumber into a warm, semiconscious state. She heard Richard moving about the cabin, his grunt of discomfort as he tried to accommodate his lean form to the narrow window seat, and his footsteps as he once again approached the bed. Her muscles tensed as she felt him climb into the bed beside her, though she kept her eyes closed. Was this the moment? Would he now assert his husbandly rights?

What should she do? How should she do it? His near-ness radiated a warmth that sorely tempted her to cuddle against the hardness of his body. Her uncertainties kept her paralyzed and she remained unmoving, pretending a sleep she was far from feeling. The hours dragged on, and still Richard did not turn to her. She rolled on her side, her back to her new husband, but the movement went unnoticed by her bedmate. Other doubts began to assail her. Why wasn't he coming to her? Was there something about her person he found undesirable?

Rose mentally chided herself. What is the matter with me? First I don't want him to come near me, now I do. I fear I am too passionate so I bury that side of me, and then I long to show him how passionate I can be. I'm far worse than any heroine in a Radcliffe novel. This is the most ridiculous situation to be in. After all, he is my husband. Many spouses know less about each other than we do when they first marry. Surely the more physical comforts of marriage help to establish the deeper, more noble foundations. But to turn to him now, without his instigation, would be conceding to those baser instincts that a gentleman would surely find abhorrent. No, he must make the first move. She waited tensely through the night for something that never came.

It was an exhausted, red-eyed Rose that watched the shore of England slip away the next morning. Richard had risen and dressed without a word to her and come out on deck before she could command her stiff body to get out of bed. He was on the deck below now, talking with Captain Deering. Tillie, in far better shape than her mistress after a good rest at the inn, stood next to Rose.

"He was ever so considerate, he was, my lady. That Mr. Hamstead, I mean, my lord's valet. Made certain I was taken care of all right and tight. I never rode in a coach for so long, my lady, and I'm afeared I got a wee bit ill. But I feel fine now."

Rose wished the little maid would stop chattering. Her head ached dully and she wanted nothing more than to be left alone. "Would you get me some tea, Tillie? I feel the need of some sustenance."

Tillie bobbed a curtsy. "Of course, my lady. The kitchen—they call it a galley, isn't that strange—is just on the lower deck. I'll fetch you some right away."

"Bring it to the cabin. I think I shall lie down for a bit. It will take us three hours to make the crossing with not much to look at except gray water and grayer skies." Rose headed for the gangway.

Richard watched Rose descend into the ship. He felt as exhausted as she looked, though years of ignoring his own discomfort kept him from showing it. He knew that he must keep all his wits about him from this point on. Even aboard ship, he must continue the charade of St. Croix lest some crafty agent of Bonaparte decides to question the crew about their employer. All angles must be considered if the mission were to succeed, and succeed it must. England must prepare herself against Bonaparte and the information he was to gather could very well make the difference between success in that endeavor or failure.

"I'll wager, Captain Deering, a hundred pounds, that you cannot make Dieppe in under three hours. And I'll throw in a guinea for each member of the crew if you do it." He arranged the top cape of his greatcoat as he spoke.

Every sailor within hearing distance raised his head and looked at their captain. With these conditions, that would be easy money, they all knew.

"Done, Lord St. Croix, and you may as well get your money pouch out now. For, with this wind and easy sea, we'll see the spires of the cathedral by ten."

The captain was as good as his word. Rose found herself disembarking from the yacht while the weak February sun was still in the east. Richard seemed in a hurry and he rushed Rose to the hired carriages that were to take them to Beauvais.

Chapter Nine

THE CONDITION OF the coaches was deplorable and the one Rose and Richard shared was permeated with a foul odor that Rose was afraid to even try to identify. To top it off, the roads were in such a state of disrepair, they were bumped and jostled from one side of the carriage to the other.

"I thought Napoleon was bringing improvements to France," Rose commented wryly.

"He is. Believe it or not, this is a vast improvement over the way this road was under the directorate. Since the Revolution, nothing gets done. Until very recently, everything was decided in committee and, thus, nothing ever got accomplished. You'll find France very confusing, my dear. They don't even date events like the rest of Europe. For instance, this is not 1803, it is Brumaire Nine. Wonderful, isn't it, that the French have the conceit to change everything solely, I'm sure, to discommode the traveler. Incidentally, my dear, do you speak French?"

Rose nodded. "It was part of the curriculum at the Bath Academy. Don't you?"

"Never quite got the hang of it. Oh, I can order a decent meal if it comes to that and make out if a merchant is cheating me, but that's the extent of it. Any more and I'm completely lost."

They came to the first of many tollgates and Rose watched as their driver handed down one of the new franc papers. "How many of these before we reach Beauvais?" she asked Richard.

"I have no idea, though I understand the number varies on any given day, depending on how enterprising one of the citizens feels like being."

Rose began to feel like Jonathan Swift's Gulliver as each amazing new event unfolded. She saw filthy laborers sporting ribbons and silver buttons on their coats while they apparently did nothing but argue. At the coach stops they were eyed suspiciously and served with a total lack of hospitality. Women were addressed as "citizeness," though the title didn't seem to raise their social status. By the time they reached Beauvais in the late afternoon, she was less than enthralled by the French people.

Matters improved a bit when the carriages deposited them at the Hotel St. Jacques on the main street of the town. Despite the revolution, this ancient hostelry managed to maintain some of its past elegance. Most of the signs of the looting and madness of the Revolution had been eliminated, though Rose noted that there was an occasional discoloration on the walls where once a painting had hung. Here, the staff addressed Richard by his English title and generally behaved in the open, friendly way that had made French hospitality so famous.

Once they were safely in their own chamber, Rose waited for an opportune moment to talk with Richard about the previous night. She felt embarrassed that she had gotten tipsy and had decided that he had been so disgusted with her, he had no desire to pursue a more intimate relationship.

"About last night," she began, but her husband interrupted her.

"Ah, yes, I must apologize for that, my dear.

Dreadfully bad idea, staying on the yacht." Richard forestalled her, not wanting to get into a deep conversation about their situation. He had work to do that night. "I think you shall be much happier here. Pity we couldn't get separate rooms. I know you would sleep much better in a bed alone."

Rose gasped, certain his barbed comments were meant to hurt her. Why else would he wish for separate beds? This was, after all, their wedding trip.

"Besides, my dear, you look fagged to death. And no wonder. That had to be the most uncomfortable coach ride since man invented the wheel. I'll have them send up a little something for you and then you can go right to bed."

"Richard, I . . ." Rose tried again.

"Want a bath. Of course, I'll order it on my way out." Richard was already picking up his coat.

"Out? You're going out? We just arrived. Certainly you must want to change."

Richard shook his head. "No time. There's a mill on the outskirts of town that I'm determined to see."

"A mill? Oh, you mean a fight. But, how did you know of such a thing?" Rose was leery of Richard's sudden haste to be gone.

"The proprietor told me," Richard said easily. "Don't wait up for me. I will probably be very late. If you need something, Hamstead will be right outside. Shall I have him send in Tillie to assist you?" Not waiting for an answer, Richard let himself out the door.

Well, of all things! Rose thought angrily. He's probably off to some brothel or gaming hell and doesn't want me to know. This cannot go on. No matter how late he is, I'll wait up for him and we will finally clear the air. She turned to her trunks and eyed them thoughtfully. She'd have a better chance of making her point with Richard, she decided, if she looked more appealing to him. There was a fine linen-and-lace peignoir among the petticoats and unmentionables Madame Vereaux had provided. Perhaps that would hold Richard's attention long enough for them to discuss their situation.

Richard found Gillis in the common room and summoned him with an imperial wave. "I'll be out for a bit, Hamstead. I plan to try my luck at the Chien Noir. I hear they usually have a decent game going on. Send the viscountess's maid to her and see to any other demands your mistress may have. Don't wait up for me. I shall be very late."

Gillis frowned. He didn't like the idea of Richard going off to a rendezvous with a contact without his backup, especially after what had happened on the ship. "But won't your lordship be needing me?"

"Nonsense, Hamstead," Richard replied in haughty tones. "Why would I need a valet at the gambling tables?"

Gillis said no more while he helped Richard on with his greatcoat.

Under his breath Richard whispered to him. "Cheer up, man. I'm just meeting our contact."

Gillis merely grunted. "Good luck, my lord," he said as he held the door open for Richard.

"Thank you, Hamstead. I'm sure the change of environ will stimulate a change in my fortune." Richard walked past him and out into the street.

Beauvais, Richard observed, was a town in transition. Here, on the main street, signs of the Revolution had all but been eradicated. The French had yet to incorporate oil street lamps, but some light was provided by the lanterns hung out by the restaurants and homes. Yet, every one of the side streets were dark alleys, left over from the medieval construction. He kept a firm hold on his sword stick as he walked up the avenue to the casino.

The Sangre de Roi had once been exclusively for the rich clientele that traveled the Paris/Dieppe Turnpike. Now, like the St. Jacques, it had been stripped of its gilt and silk, but it still bustled with the hum of roulette wheels and held that peculiar tension that occurs when a person's entire fortune lies on the turn of a card. Richard turned his greatcoat over to a man waiting in the entry and walked into the main hall.

Richard located a table in what once had been the dining room and now was serving much as a common room at an inn. He ordered a bottle of wine and a light supper and looked around him, hoping to spot his contact. Pierre Rouen was as crafty at disguise as Richard himself, and it took the Englishman a few minutes to spot the man among the other citizens. Richard allowed his eyes to slide over Rouen, not wanting anyone to see that he held any special interest in the man. When the time was right, they would make contact.

Instead, Richard focused his attention on the half-charred pullet the waiter placed before him. It had been smothered in wine sauce, no doubt to hide the blackened underside. Apparently the Revolution had reached the kitchen help. They probably held a committee meeting to see who would turn the spit, he thought wryly.

The wine was surprisingly good, and Richard carried the bottle with him back into the main salon. He tried his luck at the tables, not winning, but not really losing either. Finally a man dressed in a worn town coat and knee breeches, with the oddly shaped red hat worn by the revolutionaries cocked on the side of his head, approached him.

"Ah, you are a foreigner, here, *n'est-ce pas?*" the man said in broken English.

Richard recognized Rouen's voice at once though he gave no sign. "Maze wee, mon aimee," Richard said, making his pronunciation as bad as possible.

"You are English?"

"Yes." Richard imitated the sigh of relief of a person who had been struggling with a language they barely understood. "You speak English?"

"Mais oui. Absolument," Rouen replied in French. "You would like a little game of cards?" He ruffled the deck he held.

"Certainly, name your game."

They returned to Richard's table and Rouen offered the deck for Richard to cut. "You know how to play Les Coeurs?"

"Hearts? Of course." Richard took up the hand that was dealt to him and studied its contents. He noticed that the queen he held seemed slightly thicker than the other cards. He continued to play as if everything were normal, taking a trick with the queen and placing the small pile of pasteboards at his elbow. When the hand was over, he turned the cards over to Rouen, deftly palming the queen.

They continued, Richard receiving two more of the thicker cards in the course of the game. He switched from drinking wine to ordering brandy as he continued to lose heavily. To any observers, it seemed that one of the citizens of Beauvais had found a likely foreign pigeon and was plucking him quite nicely.

"Citizens, it is curfew," the proprietor announced in French at eleven o'clock. "By order of the Council, this establishment must close. Thank you and good night."

Although Richard had understood every word, he turned uncomprehending eyes on his companion.

Rouen's eyes held just a glint of admiration for

Richard's dissembling. "It is time to leave," he said very slowly, as if he were speaking to a half-wit.

"Really, so soon? How odd. In England we game as long as we please."

Rouen rose from the table, Gallic indignation radiating from his barrel-chested body. "You insult us, monsieur."

"I what?" Richard looked around in bewilderment. Only a few heads had turned in their direction and those quickly dismissed what they saw in their hurry to get home.

Rouen quickly gathered up his cards and turned away from Richard.

Richard continued to play the role of confused traveler as he watched the establishment's patrons take up their coats and hurry out the door. He caught the proprietor's eye and gave a helpless shrug.

That man came hurrying over and reached out to take the viscount's sleeve. He gave it a little tug and started to push Richard toward the door. *"Anglais, dépêchez-vous. C'est la curfew. La curfew."*

Richard allowed himself to be hustled through the door, barely claiming his cloak from the man in the hall as the proprietor rushed him past. All the way out he wailed his confusion, thus firmly convincing everyone within earshot he was nothing more than a foreign fool.

Back on the street, he shrugged on his greatcoat and readjusted his hat. All around him the citizens of Beauvais scurried to reach their homes before midnight lest they be caught by the watch and forced to pay a heavy fine or be imprisoned. Richard turned his own steps in the direction of the St. Jacques.

Rose allowed Tillie to brush her hair and tie it back with a blue satin ribbon for the night. Later she'd don the frilly lace nightcap that matched the robe she now wore, but for now she sat in dishabille, trying to read from the volume of William Blake poetry that Athena had given her. Her eyes barely focused on the page as her indignation over Richard's sudden departure turned into anger. Once she went to the door only to find the loyal Hamstead positioned in a chair directly across the hall.

"Are you there to keep undesirable persons away from my door, or to keep me in?" Rose asked him irritably.

Hamstead's gold tooth flashed slightly as he answered her. "My lord just wants to see to your comfort, my lady," he said, rising from his seat when he saw her. "Is there something my lady wishes?"

"No. That will be all," Rose closed the door.

Once again she tried to take up her book and read, but the paradoxical symbology of tigers and lambs was totally lost on her in her agitated state of mind. Instead, she continued to seethe at Richard's offhanded treatment of her ever since they started this trip. When she thought about the previous night, her anger took even stronger hold, though she studiously ignored any examination into why this should be so.

She was seated by the hearth when Richard finally did return. As soon as she heard the door open, she sprang up to face him.

Richard almost choked when he saw the unintentional picture Rose presented. The fire in the hearth clearly silhouetted her body through the fine lawn of her gown and robe. Her hair, unbound, caught the light and shimmered with the red sparks that fascinated him. It was highly erotic, and Richard found himself responding physically.

"You still up? I said there was no need to wait for me. You need your rest." He tried to cover his rising heat with small talk. If she'd just go to bed, he could pretend to read by the fire for a while, until the all too physical evidence of his desire subsided.

Instead, she strode toward him, stopping about three feet from his form. "Richard, where were you? There was no mill. You've been gambling again, haven't you?" Despite her efforts, she could not keep the accusatory tone from her voice.

Richard didn't pay attention to her words. He was having too much trouble controlling his response to the purely primitive allure of her soft body beneath the nightclothes. "Rose, just go to bed. We'll discuss this in the morning."

How dare he, she thought, try to send me off to bed like some troublesome child! "We'll talk now, Richard. For days I've been trying to pin you down and have a serious discussion about our future and your gambling—two items that are of the utmost importance to the both of us. Yet, you always turn any talk aside, or sneak out as you did tonight. Enough is enough. We shall have it out now!" Rose tossed her head back and glared at him defiantly. Something in his eyes made her hesitate. Was she pushing him too far? She ignored this momentary doubt and pushed on.

"Richard, have you heard anything I've said?" she asked, taking a step back from him, despite her resolve.

"I hear you," he replied in a voice as soft as velvet. He took one purposeful step toward her. "I hear you, and see you."

"Are you drunk?" Rose asked, not understanding this new side. Before he'd been aloof, conceited, and even obnoxious, but she had never seen him in this mood before. "Is that where you've been? In some tavern guzzling wine and ogling women?"

"Brandy. And I didn't guzzle. One doesn't guzzle brandy, one sips it." He was directly in front of her now. He could see the fine line of cleavage beneath the pink bow that held the thin robe closed. He stood, seemingly mesmerized by the rise and fall of her rounded breasts as she breathed heavily.

Rose refused to back off any farther. She tried to feign disgust at him, but his nearness touched a deep, hidden chord inside of her. Her knees turned to mush and there was a strange aching in her loins. Richard reached out a hand, which she feebly brushed away. "Don't touch me."

Richard ignored her halfhearted attempt and slid his hand along her shoulder until it rested on the side of her neck. "Why so angry, Rose? What have I done to deserve this treatment? Could it be something else other than my reticence? Could you desire me to stroke the nape of your neck like this?" His strong fingers gently caressed her nape.

The gesture sent delicious sensations up and down Rose's spine, further weakening her already crumbling defenses. "Please," she whispered.

"Please what?" Richard continued to massage her neck. "Please kiss me? Is that what you want, Rose?" He pulled her closer and brought his head down to hers. With the lightest touch, he kissed her eyelids and traced his lips along her cheek until he found her mouth. He pressed his own to hers, building up the intensity of the embrace by pulling her to him.

"That's not what . . ." Rose struggled to keep her equilibrium. She had had hints before of what his embrace could do to her peace of mind, but they were mere shadows of the havoc he was wreaking now. She felt him lift her in his arms and, with no conscious command from her, her arms slipped around his neck.

"Please, Richard, I'm so confused. I don't understand," she whispered in a half-choked voice, burying her face into his shoulder.

"You will, sweeting, you will," Richard whispered into her ear.

Rose heard his words and felt the caress of his breath on her ear. She became lost in the sensations, unable to resist the overwhelming desires that washed through her.

Richard carried her over to the bed and gently laid her down, stretching his long form beside her. With more kisses and strokes, he soothed away the last of her fears.

Chapter Ten

Gillis and Tillie looked at their employers the next morning and instantly knew something was afoot. Rose wore a sleepy, catlike smile that fooled no one and Richard was apt to cast contented, sidelong looks at his bride. Gillis harrumphed at all this moon-pie silliness as he held the door for the viscount to exit the inn.

"I trust everything went well last night, my lord."

Richard put on his hat and gave it a jaunty tap. "Most satisfactorily, Hamstead. Most satisfactorily."

"I can see that, my lord," Gillis said archly.

Richard ignored his remark and turned back to Rose. "Ready, my dear?"

"Coming, Richard." Rose gathered up her reticule and came over to him. "On to Paris."

The drive along the highway was little better than that of the previous day, but Rose did not seem to notice the discomforts. The experiences Richard had taught her last night gave everything a rainbow aura that changed the rutted roads and poorly sprung coaches into an exciting adventure. She couldn't help but notice Richard's glances, and she was thrilled to know that he was as strongly affected by their lovemaking as she had been. It was as if some tightly wound coil had suddenly been released inside of her and she felt buoyant and very much alive. For the moment she allowed these feelings to blot out everything else and just enjoyed the day and the company of Richard, now her husband in deed as well as on paper.

The closer they got to Paris, the more tollgates and higher charges were presented to their driver, who promptly handed them over to the viscount. It was Rose who had to try and translate what the gate men and coachman were saying at each stop.

"You speak French very well, my dear," Richard commented at one stop. Then, with a lascivious grin, he pulled her closer to him. "I have found that you do everything very well. Under my tutelage I foresee a great future for you."

"You are going to tutor me in French? How curious, since you can barely say *coq au vin*."

"I was thinking of other, more intimate lessons. You may employ French during them if you wish."

Rose chuckled. "How magnanimous of you. And when is the next lesson, my lord tutor?"

"As soon as we get to our accommodations, if you like. I've had rooms reserved at the Hôtel d'Isle. Unfortunately, Paris is very crowded at the moment and one must make do with whatever one can get."

"I'm certain it will be fine." Rose snuggled happily against his greatcoat, slipping her hand into one of its pockets for warmth. Her fingers brushed something and she pulled it out. "Richard, what's this? It looks like a playing card."

"It is a playing card." Richard hastily took it from her and put it back in his pocket. "A little souvenir, nothing more."

The evidence of his previous night's gambling cast a momentary pall over Rose's high spirits, but she quickly recovered. All that had been before Richard had shown her the mysteries of love. Surely, now, he would prefer to remain with her in the evenings and continue the "lessons" than go out and frequent the bars and gaming halls.

Richard found himself once again taking himself to task. There had been no chance to steam open the special playing cards that had been passed to him last night, what with Rose and all that followed. He must find some safe, private place to separate the cardboards and extract the information that would tell him where to make his contacts. The information he was to garner was vital to keep the French on their side of the Channel.

In mid-afternoon, their coaches rumbled through the North Gate of Paris and along the Champs-Elysées, that newest of Bonaparte's thoroughfares. It then continued into the warren of narrow streets that still remained of the old Paris. Finally it pulled up before a medieval structure of worn stone with a slightly lopsided sign that marked it as the Hôtel d'Isle.

Hardly the usual accommodations for a viscount, Rose mused as she took in the worn facade. She allowed Richard to take her hand and help her down from the carriage. There were no grooms or footmen to attend their arrival.

"Hamstead, go and secure our rooms," Richard directed.

"My lord, you can't mean here! Surely the coachman has brought us to the wrong establishment." Gillis looked around at the building and grounds. "My lord, forgive me, but 'tis no fit place for my lady and yourself."

"I fear there is no mistake, Hamstead. This was all that was available. Come, man, think of its bright points. It is conveniently located to the heart of Paris. Why, the Palais Royal can be no more than a few blocks from here." Richard's words were more than idle chatter. He was pleased with the hostelry, though not for its accommodations, but precisely because of its location. Several alleys ran along its side and back, and there was easy access to the rooftops should he have need of slipping out unnoticed. Yes, the Hôtel d'Isle would do very nicely.

The interior was somewhat better than the exterior. At least it was reasonably clean. Their rooms were located on the second floor and Rose followed the proprietor up the narrow, crooked steps to the next level.

They were shown to a two-room suite, a small sitting room with a bedroom beyond. From the innkeeper's manner, Rose could tell these were to be considered prime accommodations. Tillie and Hamstead would sleep in the garret.

The manager proudly indicated the bellpull that would ring upstairs to summon the maid and valet. "As you see," he said in broken English, "we have all the accommodations for your comfort. Our dining room is excellent, considering the times." He turned to Richard. "There have been several messages and calling cards left for you, monsieur. I shall have a boy bring them up *immédiatement*."

"Calling cards already?" Rose took off her muff and hat and turned them over to Tillie.

"Word of our arrival preceded us, evidently. Now, my sweet, what would you like to do now? You must be fagged to death after that abominable ride." Richard indicated that Gillis should begin unpacking his trunks as the hotel lackeys began carrying them through the door.

"I would very much like to have some refreshment. I fear, with all four of us in this room, it is a bit crowded and we are getting in Tillie's and Hamstead's way."

"You're perfectly correct, my dear. We'll adjourn to the dining room. Oh, Hamstead, after you finish with this, order a bath for the viscountess and myself. A good, hot, *steaming* bath."

"Very good, my lord."

Down in the dining room, Richard placed their order and accepted the notes and cards that had been waiting for them. He sifted through the stack, handing Rose those addressed to "Viscountess St. Croix" and kept the others to peruse himself.

"Here's one from the English ambassador's wife, Lady Whitworth, inviting us to a soiree this evening." Rose handed the heavy vellum card over to Richard.

"Really? Very thoughtful of her. We shall attend, of course."

"But Richard, we've just arrived!" Rose was surprised at his eagerness to enter the social whirl so soon. She had expected they would spend at least a couple of nights in their own company.

"What better way to meet our compatriots? Besides, it will give you the opportunity to meet other ladies so you will not feel so isolated on this foreign shore."

"I would not feel isolated with you here." Rose reached out to touch his hand.

Richard steeled himself against the tender feelings her touch aroused in him. He must get on with his mission. "I fear, my love, I shall not always be about. Surely you would not want me to be constantly underfoot? It is my experience, ladies find having a male hanging about all the time to be most annoying."

"As you say, Richard," Rose looked down at the croissant on her plate.

Richard heard the disappointment in her voice. "After all, my dear, we still have the entire afternoon for our private pursuits."

She raised her head and gave him a naughty little grin. "Richard, in the afternoon!"

"Why not? We're legally married." He took her hand. "By the time I'm finished with you, my dear," he said in mock-threatening tones, "you'll beg for some respite."

"Really, my lord? I must tell you, I do not succumb so easily."

"I do love a challenge," Richard said, leading her from the dining room.

Back in their room, Rose was pleased to see that Tillie had organized everything for her convenience and then withdrawn. The copper hip bath was placed before the hearth in the bedchamber with a silk privacy screen shielding it from drafts and the rest of the room. Two more cans of hot water were resting on the hearth.

"I shall need help with my buttons again, Richard." Rose presented her back to her husband and smiled coquettishly at him over her shoulder.

"Always a pleasure, my dear." He deftly undid them for her and stood back, nearly knocking the screen over.

"Richard, be careful!" Rose called out, foreseeing disaster.

Richard nimbly caught the frame and righted it. He began moving it about, adjusting it so that it curved around the tub. "I feel a nasty draft coming from the French doors, sweeting. I shouldn't want you or I to catch the influenza."

Rose removed her traveling clothes down to her petticoats. She could feel Richard's eyes on her and she smiled to herself. It was a wonderful thing, she thought, this magnetism between man and woman. But she would much rather pursue the logical conclusion after she had bathed. She slipped behind the screen before removing her unmentionables.

Richard watched her retreat without a word. It amazed him how naturally Rose played the seductress, with no conscious effort on her part, he was sure. It made his work all the more difficult. "In the water yet, love?" he called.

"Yes, and it feels divine."

"Can I get you anything?"

"Not a thing, thank you. Tillie has it all set out here by the tub."

Richard moved around to the two extra cans of hot water and lifted one of the lids. A satisfying puff of steam rose up. He turned his head slightly toward the screen that he had especially maneuvered to conceal his actions.

"Are you certain you don't need your back scrubbed?" he called out.

The sound of Rose's musical laughter answered him. He crossed over to the wardrobe and extricated the three playing cards from his coat pockets, then returned to the steaming cans. Carefully setting the first lid aside, he held the cards, one by one, over the mouth until the moisture loosened the paste that held them together. Richard then cautiously separated each one, finding the information he sought written in code on tightly folded slips of paper. He read each one, committing the contents to memory. The code was one he and Rouen had used before. His first meeting would take place two nights hence in the Bois de Boulogne. He was to wait by the big oak in the old King's Clearing at ten in the evening.

Richard frowned. He didn't like the idea of meeting in the old hunting preserve. He'd much rather meet in a lively tavern or market where the crowd provided cover for a clandestine meeting. In his experience solitary rendezvous were far too easy to spot. He'd better take Gillis as a lookout, just in case.

Taking up the false cards, he stuffed the papers back into their hiding place and tossed them into the fire.

"What are you doing?" Rose asked softly as she came from behind the screen. She had seen him throw the playing cards into the hearth.

"Just getting rid of some old souvenirs." Richard came over to embrace her. "Somehow, I no longer feel the need to hold on to them. In fact, to do so, could be quite hazardous. For, I could tell they displeased you and I want no wrathful Titania on my hands this afternoon."

"Richard, I'm no fairy queen. I'm just a flesh-and-blood woman who hopes for a loving husband and a family of her own."

"I shall dedicate myself this afternoon to convincing you that you have attained at least part of your desire." Richard stood back, still holding her hand. "But first, it is my turn in the tub."

The ambassador's soiree hardly resembled the small gathering the name originally meant, not at all, Rose thought. There were easily a hundred people there. All, it seemed, bent on meeting the Viscount and Viscountess St. Croix. To Rose's surprise and irritation, Richard practically abandoned her once they had gone through the receiving line. He had turned her over to Lady Whitworth and disappeared among the throng at the buffet table.

"Charming man, your husband," Lady Whitworth commented as she watched his tall back disappear among the crowd. "I understand you are newlyweds. Have you known the viscount long or did he sweep you off your feet?"

Rose was taken aback by the sudden personal question, but she strove to maintain the placid facade society demanded. "We were betrothed in childhood. It was all arranged by my grandfather, the late viscount."

"Oh, that quite explains it," Lady Whitworth said vaguely. "But you mustn't worry. See, already you are attracting quite a coterie of suitors." With a mischievous glint in her eye, she indicated the young men waiting for an introduction. "Not everyone here is English, mind you." Lady Whitworth began to weave a path through the anxious young men, pausing to introduce Rose to those she felt the new viscountess should know. "Allow me to introduce Signor Giorello of the Italian embassy. Now, Pietro, you must behave yourself or I shall promptly take the Viscountess St. Croix as far from you as this room will permit," Lady Whitworth teased the rather intense young man.

"Lady Whitworth, I would never do anything to cause a moment of distress for any lady, much less one of such beauty and refinement as Madame la Vicomtesse. Forgive me, Vicomtesse, but you are like a Botticelli angel. Please allow me to gaze upon your heavenly face as a supplicant gazes upon the altar."

"Phashaw, signor, do not put me up on some worshipful pedestal," Rose replied, lightly. "I do assure you, I am all too human."

"And it is that human quality that makes you all the more enticing, Madame la Vicomtesse," Giorello replied smoothly.

"Enough, Pietro." Lady Whitworth tapped him lightly with her fan. "There are several other people I wish to introduce Viscountess St. Croix to this evening."

"I must let you go then," the Italian said sadly. "But, first, permit me to call on you tomorrow. Being new to Paris, you will need someone to show you the sights. It would be my great honor to do so."

Rose shook her head. "I'm afraid tomorrow is not possible. We have only just arrived and there is so much to attend to."

"Perhaps another time, then." Giorello bowed as they passed on.

Lady Whitworth made it a point for Rose to meet everyone in the tight little English group. From the conversations, Rose learned that most of the English were uneasy about the state of affairs in France. Everywhere she heard plans to return to England being discussed. Others felt that such planning was premature, but, since Bonaparte was such a volatile character, it was best to be cautious.

"Paris is not what it once was, I'm afraid," Lady Whitworth said to Rose as they joined a group of young women about Rose's own age. After the introductions, she continued. "I lived here with my family before the Revolution. It was such a gay, gaudy city. Queen Marie Antoinette would drive through the streets in her gold-and-blue coach, on the way to one of her country outings. She had a mock farm where she would go and play at being a shepherdess, you know. It's true, the streets were narrow and unlit, but the city had a certain charm it lacks now. Bonaparte has torn up many of the old sections, for sanitation reasons, he says."

"You will find many strange things in Paris these days, Viscountess." One of the young matrons, Lady Heath, smiled at Rose. "Why, the old royal gardens are now the sites of the most disreputable businesses. Of course, it is only the east side. The west has the most exclusive shops and restaurants. A pity one gets a clear view of the other from the walks. Would you care to accompany me on a little shopping expedition tomorrow?"

"Why, thank you, Lady Heath. I should enjoy that. I'm sure the viscount has plans of his own for the afternoon and shopping with you would be a pleasant respite from all the rush of settling into our rooms."

"You're at the Hôtel d'Isle, aren't you?" Lady Heath asked. "I'll be by to fetch you about two then. Oh, we'll have such a good time!"

*   *   *

Richard, without giving any outward indication, was following Rose's progress across the room. He kept his face impassive as he saw a member of the Italian consulate fawn over her hand and forced down the feeling of jealousy that rose when he saw her smile at the fool. It was with some relief he watched her move away from the male admirers to the groups of ladies.

"I say, St. Croix, devilishly handsome wife you've got there." Lord Whitworth, England's ambassador to the court of Napoleon Bonaparte, commented. "The old viscount's granddaughter, isn't she?"

"Quite. But you were telling me about Bonaparte's Reviews. Sounds like quite a show. Something I should like to see. What would it take to get an invitation to such an event?"

"Why, I'll attend to it. Elizabeth would enjoy having the two of you along to liven up the proceedings. There's one in a fortnight that Bonaparte is particularly keen on my attending. Wants to impress me with his display, no doubt. A childish attempt to show force to win his point."

Richard wasn't so certain as the ambassador. From what he had studied of Bonaparte, it seemed the man used his famous temper and tenacity for effect, but always backed it up with real strength. "How are relations between us, Lord Whitworth? I mean, is it safe to be in Paris?"

"As safe as Hampshire, my dear viscount. Bonaparte would never dare do anything to discommode British subjects."

Richard pretended to accept the ambassador's words, but he gave the man a hard look. Lord Whitworth had the reputation of being a shrewd negotiator. Were his words simply an attempt to allay the fears of a tourist? What was really going on in the ambassador's mind?

"St. Croix, we hear you are quite a hand with a deck of cards. Why don't you join us in the side salon? Lady Whitworth has set up a few tables there. Small stuff, really." A rather florid-faced young man came up to him.

Richard remembered his name was the Honorable Sebastian Heath. "Why not? Will you excuse me, sir?" He bowed toward the ambassador.

"Go on, go on." The older man waved them away and went to talk to another young group of men over by the buffet table.

"Do you enjoy gaming, St. Croix?" Heath asked as he steered Richard toward two other men at a table in the side salon.

"Indeed, yes. And I thank fortune I have the means to support the habit. What shall we play, gentleman?"

"How about a few hands of hazard?" one of the seated pair suggested as he rose to greet them.

"Hazard it is." Richard took a seat and began shuffling the cards. He studied his companions during the play and realized they were just the type to introduce him to Madame LaRoche's establishment. It was the established contact point in Paris and if anyone needed to get a message to him, it would be sent to madame's. By being taken there, apparently at random, he would call less attention to himself. After all, he wasn't supposed to know anything about Paris.

When the game slowed, Richard looked up from his cards at his companions and threw in casually. "I say, what amusements are there in Paris these days? I expect all the fanaticism of the Revolution quite wiped out all the old delights."

Heath warmed to the topic immediately. "I should say not. Oh, the clientele is not so select anymore, but there are still plenty of diversions."

"We should take St. Croix to Le Lyon Rouge. He'd

find a bit of excitement there," Sir Robert Chaumbly, suggested.

Edward Lassiter, the third member of the group, shook his head. "Too filthy. No telling what you might catch there. How about Madame LaRoche's? It at least makes some attempt at the old elegance. The tables are only slightly bent in the house favor and the wenches are comely. Plus, she has a wine cellar that rivals Bonaparte's."

"That settles it. Madame's it is. Good wine, good women, and good gambling. What more could we ask for?" Heath sat back in his chair and drank heavily from the brandy he held. "We'll set it up."

Returning to the hotel after the party, Rose began to chastise Richard for spending the night in the card room, but thought better of it. You can catch more flies with honey, she reminded herself and began discussing the people she had met instead. "Lady Heath seems very sweet. I hope you don't mind, but she asked me to go shopping with her tomorrow afternoon. Of course, if you've made plans, I will send a note around making other arrangements."

"No, not at all. In fact, this relieves my mind as I, too, made some plans for tomorrow. It pleases me to see you making friends so quickly." Richard began to undo his cravat. "Shall I ring for Tillie?"

"It isn't necessary if you will assist me again." Rose smiled mischievously at him. Other women may attract him, she reasoned, but she had the advantage of being able to use her wiles in the bedroom. It wasn't much to build a marriage on, but it was a beginning.

Richard did the honors with alacrity and watched Rose slip behind the screen to don her nightclothes. He quickly changed himself and was waiting for her in the bed. "What did you make of the ambassador and his wife?" he asked as he held the covers back for her.

"Lord and Lady Whitworth? Well, she's a lot like Aunt Bernie. Gracious, seemingly naive, but she's far more aware of her surroundings than she lets on. Lord Whitworth, now, is an enigma. I think he is very worried about something and is compensating for it by being a bit blusterous." Rose snuggled against his shoulder.

"That is very astute of you, my dear. I think the ambassador is a man on the edge, waiting to see what Bonaparte will do next. It cannot be a comfortable position." He kissed her lightly on her nose. "But I would hardly call your Aunt Bernie naive. She quite raked me over the coals on more than one occasion."

"That was because she thinks you are a gambler and a wastrel," Rose informed him, a slight curve appearing at the corner of her mouth.

"But, my dear, I am. I thought you knew that," Richard assured her.

Rose just snuggled deeper into his shoulder. No, Richard, she thought. You may have been. But I intend to change all that. It may take time. But I can be very patient. Very patient indeed.

Chapter Eleven

THE SHOPPING DISTRICT of Paris rang with the sounds
of barter. Rose was amazed to find that everyone
seemed engaged in the business of trade. A woman
approached her demanding to know if she would care
to see her collection of shawls from Calais, or some
soaps from Lyons. The woman explained that she
would gladly accept some English cheese or wool in
trade.

"Is it always like this?" Rose asked Lady Heath as
they pulled away.

"It used to be far worse. For a time, everyone was
bent on making a fortune in commerce. Items that
had been looted from the grand houses during the
Revolution turned up in the open market on the Left
Bank. Everyone did it, no matter what station one
held." She picked her way daintily around a beggar
with no legs.

Rose started to give the poor man something, but
her companion forstalled her.

"Bonaparte has forbidden begging in the streets.
He has provided hospitals and homes for the veter-
ans of the Revolution. That man need only to go to
one of them and he will be cared for."

"I see." Rose looked around her at the colorful
scene. It was a far cry from what she had imagined

Paris to be like. The ancient, graceful curves of the Promenade were still there, but the people strolling under it were a hodgepodge of humanity ranging from city officials to mud-specked laborers. Everywhere she heard the greeting of "Liberty, Citizen" being exchanged. She gave a start when a man, nearly bumping into her, addressed her as "citizeness."

What shocked her the most was the apparel of the French women. Here it was, late February, and these women wore nothing more than a thin muslin chemise with tiny cap sleeves that looked as if they were cutting off circulation. To Rose's amazement, they didn't seem to be wearing much else underneath. One lady arrived at the Promenade in great estate. When she climbed down from the carriage, Rose saw she had nothing under her gown except a strange bodysuit that fit so snugly it left nothing to the imagination.

"That is Madame Tallien," Lady Heath whispered. "She's very powerful, even if she is estranged from the court."

"Why is that?" Rose asked as they turned toward a lace shop.

"She used to be one of Josephine Bonaparte's closest friends. They were imprisoned together during the Terror. But Bonaparte has decided that madame is a poor influence on his wife and forbidden her admittance to the Tuileries."

"Is the first consul always so arbitrary?"

"It would seem so, though one can never be certain. What do you think of this baby's cap? Would it not go well with this gown?"

Rose put all thoughts of politics out of her mind as she bent her attention to helping her companion make her purchases.

They paused to rest at a small café, taking up seats just one row away from the window. Neither woman could overcome her English training to sit where they could be ogled from the street, though many of the window seats were occupied by Frenchwomen. They looked at the conservatively dressed Viscountess and Lady Heath and giggled rudely.

"I fear we are considered *très gauche*, Viscountess. If you wish to be considered in fashion, I'm afraid you will have to patronize either Mademoiselle Nancy or Madame Raimbaut, depending on whether you wish to dress Greek or Roman."

Rose looked at the thin costumes dubiously. "What is the difference?"

"Lawks, I cannot tell. Perhaps the Roman is a bit more ornate."

"Don't they freeze? Or is it simply a case of anything for fashion?"

" 'Tis damaging to the health. There have been cases of young ladies expiring from the influenza they have contracted because of their mode of dress."

The ladies finished their tea and rolls and Lady Heath gathered up the small parcel she had deigned to carry herself. Rose let her gaze drift across the small garden to the more disreputable section of the Palais Royal. Her eyes narrowed as she saw a dark-clad figure swagger between the wooden posts that marked the entrance to that district. The form was tall and lean, dressed like a laborer in a knit cap and tunic. She could not see the face at this distance, but she was struck by a feeling of familiarity with the figure. Why did she think she knew a French worker? Perhaps it was someone she had seen around the hotel. Dismissing the feeling, Rose turned to assist the baroness.

"Did you see someone you know?" Lady Heath asked.

"I thought so, but was mistaken. Shall you be attending Madame Cambaceres's fete tonight? We received the invitation somewhat late, but the viscount wishes to attend."

"Yes, we shall be there. An invitation from Bonaparte's second in command is not to be ignored."

The ladies returned to their carriage. As they made the short drive back to the Hôtel d'Isle, Rose looked out on the near-chaos that was Paris and wondered how the people could survive. No wonder Bonaparte, with his reforms and dictates on social order, was so popular. These people needed direction, and they looked to the volatile First Consul to provide it.

Richard signaled for Gillis to wait by a tree several yards from the rendezvous spot. It wouldn't do for his contact to think he had brought anyone when the directions expressly dictated against it. Still, this meeting had all the earmarks of a possible trap, and Richard wanted as much of an edge as possible.

He pulled the plain publican's cape closer around him, concealing the evening dress he wore beneath. It hadn't been easy slipping out of Cambaceres's little get-together without calling attention to himself. Fortunately the residence had been on the outskirts of the city, closer to the Bois de Boulogne than Richard had any reason to hope. Hopefully he could complete this meeting and slip back into the house without anyone being aware of his absence. Of course, there was Rose. But he had left her so surrounded by fawning *cicesebos*, he doubted she would even notice he was gone.

His spine stiffened as he heard a branch crack behind him. Turning to face the sound, he positioned himself behind the trunk of the huge oak tree. Better to ascertain that this was his contact before showing himself.

The newcomer was also heavily cloaked and his

hat was pulled low over his face. When he drew even with the oak, he whispered in English, "There can be no true liberty under a dictator."

Richard replied in Gascon French, "And that dictator is Napoleon."

"We have not long, my friend," the informant said in French. "I have little to pass on to you. Just that troops are being massed in Bologne. Bonaparte ordered Colonel Rasmier to relocate his troops at the garrison there just yesterday. It is expected that he will send Junot to oversee the situation, though that is not definite at the moment."

"How many troops?" Richard asked. He caught a glimpse of the officer's uniform under the cape as his contact shrugged.

"Three regiments that I know of. Possibly four. From Bologne they can reach the Channel in three days with a forced march."

Richard doubted that Bonaparte would tramp his men through the heart of France on a secret raid. More likely he would move them to the nearest port and put them on ships. Bologne! That would give him and his superiors a starting point to deduce Bonaparte's plans. He asked a question that had been nagging at him. "Just why are you doing this?"

"Because my family was killed in the Terror. My sister was murdered by Tallien. This Corsican pretends to want to establish order and equality. He offers commissions to the sons of the old families. He hints at giving back our own land. The only family I have left is my nephew, a boy of twelve! He is in England. I do not want to lose him if Bonaparte raids your island."

Richard listened to this impassioned speech, told with typically Gallic fervor and gestures. Once he glimpsed the insignia of a captain in Bonaparte's own household guard. Should he trust this man? He had been a source of reliable information in the past.

Yet, Napoleon's influence on his staff was near-magical. This captain could have just as easily been planted to root out any resistance.

"How shall I contact you again?" the captain was asking.

"Leave word at Madame LaRoche's for L'Anglais. I will receive it."

"As you will."

Richard waited until the man was completely out of sight before stepping away from the tree. He returned to Gillis by a circumvented route, finding his old friend sitting in a thicket.

"Nary a peep all night," Gillis informed him.

"Just the way I like it," Richard replied lightly. They started back toward the built-up area. "What was that?" He heard hoofbeats some distance away.

"More than likely some late party goer. And you'd better be getting back to your fancy party. That blamed curfew is coming up."

"You're right. I'll just make it in time to say my good nights."

Rose was acutely aware that Richard was no longer in the main throng of the party. The last she had seen of him he had been in deep conversation with yet another scantily dressed French beauty. When she looked again, he was gone. She could only conclude that he had sought more private conversation with the blonde.

Not that she didn't have her own share of admirers. Few males in the room failed to remark on the viscount's disinterest in his own lovely wife. Such a situation made a woman vulnerable, and there were men enough who were willing to take advantage of that vulnerability. Rose found herself the object of attention from Edward Lassiter and Pietro Giorello, both seemingly bent on outdoing the other to win her attention.

In the course of the evening, Rose had the opportunity of viewing, firsthand, the acknowledged beauty of the Bonaparte family, Pauline Bonaparte Leclerc. Known as the "Pocket Venus," this vivacious and spoiled sister of the First Consul accepted the adulation of those present as her due. When Rose was presented to her, the Corsican beauty smiled pertly.

"Ah, another English visitor. Madame la Vicomtesse must come to our little gathering next week, Joseph," she addressed her brother who was acting as her escort.

"I shall see that an invitation is issued immediately, Madame la Vicomtesse." Joseph Bonaparte bent over Rose's hand.

It seemed she was fortunate indeed since few English received such an invitation.

"No offense meant, Viscountess," Edward Lassiter spoke up, "but I'd wager a golden boy it's because of your title. The Bonapartes have been amazingly title conscious of late, particularly for a family that arose to power on the slogans of the Revolution. You must go, of course. The first consul would make it an international incident if you did not."

Amabassador Whitworth agreed. "Indeed, Bonaparte is just looking for an incident to point the international finger at England. I'm sure you've heard of his claims that we are harassing French ships."

"If the invitation is forthcoming, I shall, of course, attend," Rose assured the ambassador. She didn't particularly like the idea of being drawn into the diplomatic game being played in Paris at the moment. Still, she was English, and attending Madame Pauline Leclerc's party was the least she could do for her country.

"Excuse me, Madame la Vicomtesse, the viscount

wishes a word with you in the side parlor." A servant politely intruded on ther conversation.

"Now, I wonder what St. Croix could want. Would you excuse me?"

"Allow me to escort you to your husband." Lassiter offered his arm.

Taking it, Rose smiled her gratitude.

They found Richard seated on a marble bench in a corner. He rose uncertainly to his feet. "Ready to go, my dear? Party's become a devilish bore."

Rose, seeing his condition, hurried forward. "Mr. Lassiter, would you see to having our carriage brought around. I should like to get the viscount out with a minimum of fuss."

"Of course." The young man hurried off.

"Richard, I've never seen you this way. The champagne at home had no such affect." Rose reached out a tentative hand to steady her husband.

"Nonsense. Champagne had nothing to do with it." He teetered precariously. "Must say our farewells."

"I'll ask Mr. Lassiter to do that for us," Rose hastened to say.

"Nonsense. Very bad manners to leave without thanking the host. Very bad manners." Richard began to weave toward the main salon.

Rose was left to trail helplessly after him. She tried to ignore the half-hidden smirks and cutting comments as she followed Richard through the room. Finally he reached Monsieur Cambaceres.

"I fear we must leave, monsieur. Thank you for the invitation." Richard hiccuped throughout this little speech, covering his mouth politely each time he did so.

The second consul was amazed. He merely looked down his rather considerable nose at the vicinity of Richard's cravat.

"Come, my dear. Time to go." Richard turned abruptly and grabbed Rose's arm.

"Merci, monsieur, madame," Rose managed to get out before Richard's insistent tugging forced her away.

He led her into the vestibule where a servant waited with their cloaks. Rose pulled away from Richard and allowed the footman to drape the pelise over her shoulders. She said not a word to him until they were esconced in their carriage and headed back to the Hôtel d'Isle.

"Richard, how could you? The second consul now will believe more than ever that we English are a rude, boorish race."

"Nonsense. He was convinced of it long ago. Don't be angry with me, Rose." Richard tried to coax her into a better mood by tickling her earlobe.

"Richard, stop that! I am very vexed with you. First you disappear from the party and then you nearly insult the host. It was too bad of you."

"Did you miss me, my thorny Rose?" He went back to stroking her ear, ignoring Rose's attempts to brush his hand away.

"Of course I missed you. How could I not, with everyone making veiled allusions to your disappearance."

Richard stopped tickling her ear at that. "Who?" he asked a shade too sharply.

Rose noticed that he didn't slur the word either. In fact, his pronunciation seemed to be getting clearer by the minute. "What is sobering you up so quickly?" she asked suspiciously.

"It must be the cool night air. Now, who noticed I was absent?"

"Well, they didn't exactly say that. It was more a case of 'Where has the viscount gone off to? I saw him come in, so he must be somewhere about.' That sort of thing. Why, what makes it so important?"

"It isn't important. But it pleases me that you missed me, though I was never far away. Just in the next room, sampling Cambaceres's cellar."

Rose was about to argue, for she had visited the supper room on more than one occasion and there had been no St. Croix. *He must think me a simpleton if he expects me to believe such an obvious lie. Very well, let him keep his secrets. I saw him with that blond woman. The rest is self-explanatory.*

The next two weeks Rose saw little of Richard. He would escort her occasionally, but more often turn that office over to Edward Lassiter or Pietro Giorello. These two young men were more than delighted to fulfill the office. Sometimes Richard would leave his man Hamstead to attend Rose and carry her packages. Rose gradually became an established part of the English community's social set. But she always looked for Richard and rarely found him. Her hurt and frustration grew. Under her facade of uncaring indifference Rose grew angrier at Richard's confusing behavior and her own inability to deal with it.

The vouchers for Bonaparte's first Review of the Season arrived, complete with instructions for proper attire. Civilian gentlemen were to dress in morning coats of either black or dark blue, with white small clothes and cravat. The ladies were to wear only white, with a pastel sash of blue, pink, or yellow being permissible.

As they were getting ready for this event, Rose took the opportunity to try to find out about her husband's activities.

"Richard, I heard an amusing rumor last night at Madame Leclerc's concerning you. Something about a race along the Avenue de Boulogne. The narrator claimed that you and your adversary carried two, uh, women the entire length of the boulevard. I was asked to confirm the rumor. Of course I denied it."

Richard paused only momentarily in adjusting his boot. "As if I would do something like that. Quite spoil the fit of my jacket."

"That's what I thought. Yet the narrator was most insistent. He said you wagered a large sum on the outcome."

"Rose, I'm surprised at you, listening to such gossip. Worse yet, allowing it to be repeated within your hearing."

"Most of it was related in French. The storyteller was assuming, no doubt, that I didn't speak the language. It was only when Madame Leclerc asked me about it that I gave it any notice."

"Ah, the fair Pauline. How she does like to twist the knife. Never mind, my sweet, it has nothing to do with you."

"Richard, you keep saying that. But, the fact of the matter is, it has everything to do with me. I just don't understand what is going on. Since we arrived in Paris, you've kept me on such a teeter-totter of emotions, I scarcely know if I'm coming or going."

"We are definitely going, or we shall never be admitted." Richard took up his coat from the bed. "Why the devil did I give Hamstead today off of all days?"

"I expect you lost track of the dates. Alcohol can do that sometimes," Rose added dryly.

The Viscount and Viscountess St. Croix sat on the wooden benches provided for those fortunate enough to hold a pass for the famous Review. With them were the Heaths, Edward Lassiter, and the British ambassador and his wife. They were waiting for the family of the first consul to arrive.

"I fear, my dear Elizabeth, we shall soon have to relocate to the dais. The first consul was most particular that we take our place there." He turned to the men in the group. "Frankly, I am dubious of the honor."

"What could he possibly do so publicly?" Heath asked.

"What could he not do? Bonaparte seems to think he is a law unto himself. He is a master of public display. It is one of the things that makes him so dangerous. Like the Corsican he is, he offers his right hand to shake while the left holds a knife." Lord Whitworth shook his head as he led his wife away.

" 'Tis the lot of the diplomat to always anticipate the worst." Richard tried to make light of the exchange.

"Oh, look, Madame Bonaparte has arrived." Matilda Heath nodded toward the carriage that was depositing the first consul's wife and mother at the parade ground.

Once the ladies had been established, a band struck up a martial tune and the Review began. The foot soldiers took up their ranks in crisp military position, followed by the cavalry. When the regiments were in position, Bonaparte came riding forth on a white Arabian horse whose coat shone brilliantly even in the rather watery March morning sun. He cantered before his troops, inspecting the ranks, then rode up to the dais where Josephine waited. Dismounting, he made his way to her side.

Taking this as their cue, the band struck up "Les Marseilles" and the troops paraded past their commander. Rose saw General Junot, in his position as commander of Paris, lead his regiment past the reviewing stand. Rose pointed him out to Richard, adding, "I have met his wife at Madame Leclerc's."

"We are expected to take refreshment under that pavilion after this is all over. I understand there will be a reception line." Lassiter indicated a red-and-white-striped awning set up not far from the reviewing stand. "Are you prepared to meet the little colonel himself, Viscountess?"

"Indeed, I am looking forward to it." Rose replied. "It is time I saw this lion whose roar everyone quakes before."

"Spoken like a true Englishwoman. But be careful. Bonaparte has been known to devour pretty women, and do worse if they reject him," Heath warned her.

The Review over, their party made its way to the tent and whatever refreshment awaited inside. Rose waited patiently beside Richard as the line moved slowly forward. Lord and Lady Whitworth were just ahead of them.

They had just reached the beginning of the receiving line where General and Madame Junot did the honors when Rose heard a hushed intake of breath come down the line. She looked up and saw that Bonaparte had turned his back on the British ambassador, ostensibly to confer with a young aide. Lord Whitworth, summoning what dignity he could, took his wife's arm and led her from the pavilion.

"Richard, perhaps we should go." Rose laid her hand lightly on his arm.

"Nonsense. That's all politics. Everyone knows I'm not the least political. Come along, my dear. The first consul awaits." He guided her along the line.

Rose wondered at Richard's insistence. Behind them the Heaths, who had yet to start along the long line of introductions, turned and followed the ambassador and his wife. Rose felt it would be far more appropriate for them to join the little band of retreating English.

Richard had other thoughts. Privately he seethed at the cavalier treatment of the representative of his country, but he also saw it as an opportunity to further establish in the mind of the French the Viscount St. Croix's total disinterest in affairs of state. Besides, he wanted to see what this man Bonaparte looked like up close.

At first glance Richard was disappointed. Bonaparte was a small man, with a receding hairline and little remarkable about him. It was only when Richard looked into his eyes that the man's power became apparent. Charisma poured forth from those eyes, drawing a man's soul into service. No wonder men will die for him, Richard thought. This is a dangerous, ambitious man.

For his part the First Consul did no more than acknowledge the viscount and viscountess with a nod, though his eyes remained overlong on Rose's cleavage. She and Richard moved on into the refreshment area.

"I should like to leave now, Richard." Rose accepted the punch he offered without tasting it. She felt awkward and angry after the incident between Bonaparte and Lord Whitworth. "We are the only English to have remained."

"Of course we can go, my pet. I have seen everything I came to see." Richard took her arm and escorted her from the pavilion.

Chapter Twelve

Rose HANDED HER small parcel over to Hamstead as he waited by the carriage in front of Madame Raimbaut's exclusive establishment. It amused Rose that, in a country flaunting its equality, snobbery ran so rampant. Madame Raimbaut was the genius behind the current passion for Roman dress among the ladies of French society. Rose had come to her in an act of desperation.

What is good for the gander is good for the goose, she thought, altering the old adage. She watched as Hamstead loaded the boxes of her new gowns into the boot of the cabriollet Richard had rented for her. Such thoughtfulness as this clashed with his open flirtations and long absences. He took every care of her, yet did it with such apparent indifference it made Rose feel as if she were some maiden aunt he was responsible for. *Let us see how he likes his wife parading around the same way, as that Madame Duvalier he seemed so drawn to the other night.* Rose thought of the object of Richard's latest dalliance, General Vidoq's latest mistress. *I should never try such tactics in England,* she continued to muse, *but Paris seems to have a way of changing one's perspectives.*

There was yet another night at the L'Opera Français followed by a supper party at some grand house to look forward to. Rose was frankly bored with the endless round of social engagements. Yet she could hardly stay in the hotel while Richard gallivanted all over Paris. She had too much pride for that. Besides, it would give her the chance to begin her new campaign to attract her husband's attention. Richard had reluctantly agreed to attend the opera, but insisted she find someone else to take to the Italian embassy for the supper party. Rose had found Pietro Giorello more than willing to fulfill that role.

Rose disliked using the young Italian in this manner, but she saw no other way. On more than one occasion she had tried to get Giorello to turn his attentions elsewhere, but he would only laugh and tell her there was no one else worthy of his attentions.

Tillie was waiting for her back at her rooms.

"My lady, the viscount sent word that he would be late and you should go on to the opera without him." The little maid began to put away Rose's new purchases.

"And just how am I to do that, without an escort?" Rose asked to no one in particular. Then, seating herself at the little desk in the front room, she wrote a brief note to Pietro Giorello. "Tillie, fetch Hamstead for me, please. I have a note I wish him to deliver."

The valet arrived and Rose gave him the missive to deliver to the Italian embassy. In it she had requested for Giorello to act as her escort to the theater. If Richard thought she would just sit at home, he had another thing coming! This only strengthened her resolve to put her new plan into action.

Rose strode purposefully toward the wardrobe and surveyed her new acquisitions. "I'll wear the white muslin with the silver embroidery, Tillie."

"Yes, my lady. And what petticoat shall you want with it?"

"No petticoat, Tillie. Madame Raimbaut designed a special *chemise classique* to wear underneath." Rose indicated the curious bodysuit that lay among her new lingerie. "And Tillie, no corset. Madame says it spoils the natural lines of the gowns."

Rose could see the little maid was shocked, but she didn't care. She would show Richard that she could compete with any of the French beauties when it came to displaying her charms.

Richard, in his Dupris disguise, was currently in deep conversation with an old woman who still remembered the glories before the Revolution. She had been a nanny in the house of the Marquis Jeraux, and she was now happily reminiscing about the old days.

"Yes, my good woman. But you have a message for me. From your grandniece, you said. Madame Duvalier."

"Oui, monsieur," the old woman cackled. "Marie has done very well for herself. Oh, if she had only been a little older, she would have attached the marquis himself. Still, she is now a lady. But she remembers. She remembers all. When the Jeraux family went to the guillotine, she wept, child that she was. You see, *le petit count* was her playmate. Eight she was, he only nine. And they took his head. *Mon petit, mon pauvre petit.*"

"You have my sympathies, Grandmother. But the message?" Richard was growing impatient. This unexpected meeting had made it impossible for him to go to the theater with Rose. If he could finish up here, he could join her by the first intermission.

"Marie said that she has some very important information, but that she cannot meet with you alone. She wants you to be on the Promenade at four, when all the carriages are out."

"She wants me to meet with her in broad daylight while all of Paris looks on?" Richard asked incredulously. Then the audicity of the plan caught his fancy. "Very well, I shall be there. Tell your grandniece to look for a lieutenant of the Guard from Bordeaux. *Au revoir, grandmère.*"

By the time Richard reached the opera house, it was well into the second act. He remained in the foyer until the intermission, then sought out Rose in the box he had reserved. The sight that greeted him disturbed him greatly. Doubly so, since he had brought it on himself.

Rose was surrounded by seven young bucks, Edward Lassiter among them. And no wonder they surrounded her like dogs on a deer. She was dressed in a gown so sheer that the soft curves of her body were clearly visible through the fabric. As he got closer, he could see that the fine convent lace of her chemise showed plainly through the muslin. Angry that anyone but he should feast his eyes on her charms, and even angrier because he could do nothing to prevent it, Richard stalked into the box.

"My dear, I had no idea you had decided to join the ranks of Paris's vestal virgins," he said dryly, eyeing her garb.

"Ah gentlemen, you must make way. My husband deigns to join us." Rose haughtily said, raising her chin in defiance toward Richard. She sensed that, despite his offhanded manner, he was seething, and that gave her some satisfaction. Still, it also made him unpredictable. No matter what else Richard was, he was no fool, and she was learning that the particular type of disinterest he now exhibited covered a very devious and calculating mind.

"Would you care for me to fetch you a strong rum

punch, my dear? It would seem you are in need of something to keep you warm." Richard ignored the others around them and looked deeply into Rose's eyes. What he saw there didn't reassure him. There wasn't a hint of contrition or uncertainty.

"No thank you, St. Croix. I am quite comfortable. Will you be staying until the end or is there a pressing game somewhere?" Rose looked him straight in the eyes.

"Shortly, my dear. But I shall stay awhile, if for no other reason than to see these young fools fall all over you," he said only loud enough for Rose to hear. "What's the matter, Rose? Do you find my caresses so chilling you seek diversion among these jackanapes?"

"Your embraces are adequate enough, such as they are," Rose whispered back, wanting to wound him. "But they are so haphazardly given, I must find some way to fill the time in between."

Jealousy, like a hot blade, slashed through Richard. Never had he thought that Rose could hurt him this badly, yet he wanted to crush her to him and drive all thoughts of another man from her mind. He wanted to punish her as she was punishing him. "You can dance naked down the Champs-Elysées, my dear, and it would still not alter the fact that you are mine. And, as I told you before, I do what I will with what is mine."

A frisson of fear ran down Rose's spine as she heard these threatening words. She began to doubt her plan and heartily wish she had never ventured out in the revealing gown.

Richard could stand watching the other men ogle his wife no longer. He stood up right in the middle of the aria and turned to the group. "Gentlemen, there is a deck of cards waiting for me at Madame LaRoche's. I leave my wife in your tender care." He was pleased that he was able to keep the sarcasm hidden in his voice. With a curt bow, he left the box.

Rose followed his exit with her eyes, then turned to face the others. She raised her chin even higher, gritting her teeth to keep the tears that threatened from spilling out. Richard had quite literally thrown her to the wolves.

The next morning, Rose and Richard sat across from each other at the breakfast table. Undercurrents of emotional electricity coursed between them, but neither made reference to the previous night.

"What are your plans for the day, Rose?" Richard asked casually. He still seethed from Rose's display, but he was bent on not showing it.

"Nothing of any importance. I am invited to a luncheon at Lady Whitworth's. Just the usual routine, I suppose."

"Could it be that Paris is already losing its charms for you, my pet?"

"You must admit it is wearying. Here it is, the first of April, and I have yet to see any of the antiquities of the city, though few enough of them remain. Paris seems so dizzingly determined to establish society. Yet, the people in position to direct these efforts are themselves socially inept. They do not seem to understand what society is all about. Rather, they are like children, playing at manners." Rose prattled on, anxious to discuss anything but the real problem between them.

"How observant of you." Richard's voice sounded stilted. "Bonaparte wants very badly to have a social structure. He believes it is necessary for the welfare of the country, and he's right. Liberty and equality are all very fine, but men need something to strive for and society provides that goal. Also, when all is said and done, Bonaparte thinks of himself as a Caesar."

"I think you are right." Rose considered throwing the sugar bowl at him to break this too-polite stalemate. But she was a civilized young woman and she passed it to him instead. "Everything he has been doing lately seems directed at some kind of imperial structure. It is said he wants to marry his sister to the Borghese prince and thus ally himself with old royalty. Could it be he is trying to get the old families of Europe to support his cause?"

Richard was once again reminded of Rose's powers of observation and deduction. It also underscored the vast chasm that stretched between him and his wife. He had spent the previous night wavering between the realization that he had come to love this woman passionately and anger that he could do nothing at present to make her love him in return. The frustration turned to anger and, characteristically, he channeled that toward accomplishing his mission. Only one more meeting after this one with Madame Duvalier and he and Rose could return to England. There, he vowed he'd try to pull their relationship out of the mire of misunderstanding and deception he was forced to maintain.

Just as in London, anyone with pretentions to society made an appearance in the Promenade during the fashionable hours between four and six o'clock. Because of the shortage of suitable carriages, more walked than rode, but this merely allowed for a greater chance to show off their clothes. To Rose, they looked like a troop of preening peacocks, bobbing in bows as they noticed an acquaintance and strutting along in their fine feathers.

She had thought that a drive in the warm April air would help alleviate the depression that had been on her since last night. The jonquil gown she now wore was a far cry from the scandalous muslin she had donned to make Richard jealous. That dress now lay crumpled in the corner she had thrown it upon her return. After the disastrous interview with Richard at the opera, she had vowed to forsake all such ploys. If he could not accept her as she was, then the devil take him. The strained conversation of that morning had only added to her moroseness.

In an attempt to lighten her mood, she turned her attention back to her escort. Giorello was wearing a coat cut in the latest fashion trend. It made him look like he had gone three rounds and lost at a mill. Rose had tried hard not to laugh when she first saw him.

"There is Monsieur and Madame Cambaceres," Pietro whispered to her as their coached passed an impressive landau.

Rose nodded a greeting to the couple, which they returned regally. It seemed everyone was bent on being seen this April afternoon. Another carriage caught Rose's eye. Its sole occupant was a voluptuous woman holding a delicate parasol of white lace and pink ribbons to protect her delicate complexion from the sun. "That is Madame Duvalier," Pietro identified the carriage's occupant for Rose.

But Rose already knew the woman's identity. Richard had fawned all over her at the Cambacereses' soiree. She barely noticed when the traffic got so thick their carriage was stalled at an intersection. Madame Duvalier's coach was similarly detained on the street to Rose's right. Madame Duvalier, Rose knew, was the mistress of the commander of Bonaparte's house guard, so it came as no surprise when she saw a lieutenant of that group ride up to the woman's coach. As the officer doffed his hat in deference to the lady, Rose drew in a sharp breath. Despite the small mustache and heavier eyebrows, Rose recognized her husband.

What is Richard up to? she asked herself, her eyes narrowing as she watched her husband play the role of a French subaltern. Why such a charade? She saw Madame Duvalier engage Richard in conversation. There is more here than a philandering husband, she told herself. Rose's mind turned back to the other times she had seen Richard act strangely, and his many absences. Up to now she had assumed he had been gambling, but a new thought struck her. Could he be involved in something far more dangerous? Rose was distracted from her thoughts when she noticed that Giorello was studying the Duvalier carriage rather intently. Richard did not want to be recognized, Rose reasoned and sought some way to distract Pietro from scrutinizing the lieutenant too closely. She dropped her parasol so that it fell on the poor man's head and then strove to recapture it, leaning across him to do so.

Giorello's gaze feasted on the rich display of her creamy breasts. His eyes fixed on the rise and fall of those soft mounds as Rose pretended to scramble for her parasol.

As she grabbed the handle, she sat up again, knocking Pietro in the nose with her gloved hand. "Oh, Pietro, how clumsy of me!" She began to pat his face in concern. "Let me look at it. Poor thing. I don't think it will swell. But perhaps we should go back to the hotel and put a compress on it. Driver, take us back to the Hôtel d'Isle."

As Richard was bowing over the hand of Madame Duvalier, he caught Rose's performance out of the corner of his eye. Now, what is that woman doing? he asked himself, even as he rose and smiled graciously at his contact.

Madame Duvalier returned his smile and accepted the missive he presented. She pretended to read the blank piece of paper, then slipped it into her décolletage, knocking her fan from her lap as she did so. Richard leaned down from his horse and retrieved the fan, presenting it to the lady with a flourish. In the process he deftly palmed the small slip of paper that had been placed between the sticks.

"Tell the general I will be most pleased to see him," Madame Duvalier said in dismissing tones.

"Certainly, madame," Richard replied in Gascon French and bowed as her carriage moved on.

Now, where is that minx? Richard asked himself as he looked around for Rose. But her carriage was turning out of the Promenade and he could not pursue it without calling attention to himself. She'd have some explaining to do tonight, Richard promised himself. What did she mean by throwing herself all over that Italian in plain view of all of Paris?

He forced himself to ride casually along the thoroughfare for all the world to see, like a young bachelor officer in no hurry to return to his duties. To do anything else would call too much attention to his actions.

When he reached the edge of the fashionable section, he turned down a side street and then another. He finally dismounted and turned the reins of the horse over to the waiting Gillis.

"Mission successful, Major?" Gillis asked.

"Yes, very. Gillis, Rose was there, with that Italian, Giorello. She behaved most peculiarly."

"How so, sir?"

"She threw herself all over the man, and in plain view of everyone on the Promenade. This presents a real kettle of fish. I can't have her making a public display of herself like that."

"What need it concern you, Major? After all, you wanted her to seem the unhappy wife of a gambling husband. Sounds to me, she is playing the part well."

Gillis looked hard at his friend. "If'n I didn't know better, I'd say all that talk about not letting her influence you on this mission is a crock."

"Your eyes are too sharp by half, my friend. But what to do? I can't let her completely ruin her reputation because of my seeming indifference."

"Are you certain that's what it is? Might be something more subtle. The viscountess is a downy one, for all she's been a bit isolated." Gillis tied up the cavalry horse Richard had ridden and went to bring over the gray St. Croix rode as the viscount.

"What else could it be? No, Gillis, it is time for St. Croix to take a firm hand with his wandering wife."

Rose managed to send Giorello on his way with a cold compress held to his nose. The fashion-conscious young man insisted that the top be put up on the carriage before he would venture out. Rose watched the closed conveyance turn the corner from her window. Now that Giorello was out of the way, she had some serious thinking to do.

Why was Richard posing as a member of Bonaparte's house guard? What could make a man don such a disguise? Was it the first time he had done so or had he hidden his identity before?

And there was Hamstead. Somehow, the valet was too correct. He seemed more like an actor playing the part than a real manservant. A valet with a gold tooth who dyed his hair—very curious indeed. And why did there seem a strange familiarity about Richard and Gillis, as if she had met them somewhere earlier.

The truth struck her suddenly and she began to smile. She was still smiling when Richard came into their bedchamber.

"Rose, I believe we need to have a talk," Richard said in tones that sounded officious even to himself.

Rose continued to smile at him. "Of course, Richard," she said mildly. "But, perhaps you'd like some brandy first." She went to pour him a glass and handed it to him. "Go ahead, take a sip. You seem a bit overwrought."

Richard eyed Rose suspiciously, but took a swallow from the glass.

"Tell me, Richard, how long have you been a spy?" Rose asked sweetly.

Chapter Thirteen

THE BRANDY SPEWED from Richard's mouth as he choked at Rose's words. "Whatever put that fancy in your head?" he said, mopping the front of his coat with a handkerchief.

Rose was thoroughly enjoying herself. Richard would never have reacted that way if she weren't right. "Oh, come now, Richard. It was obvious. Of course, when I realized you were also the longshoreman who rescued us on the Guildford Highway, everything became clear."

Still cautious, Richard eyed her speculatively. "And how did you reach that conclusion?"

"Well, to be honest. I realized that Hamstead was the older rescuer first. He's not really your valet, is he? He's your accomplice, or co-spy, or whatever you call them."

"You still haven't answered my question."

"Hamstead has a gold tooth and dyes his hair. The only other person I have ever met with a gold tooth in that same position was the older longshoreman. Also, he seemed to disappear quite as much as you did." Rose began to warm to her topic. "Of course, I didn't put all this together until I saw you today on the Promenade. Even that false mustache and eyebrows could not disguise your lean form, my love."

Richard tried to ignore the pleasurable sensation Rose's endearment caused in him and remain stern. "Me, in the Promenade?"

Rose began to lose patience. "Yes you, talking with Madame Duvalier. And I suspect that you may have been a laborer I saw slipping into the disreputable side of the Palais Royal. I also suspect that this gambling, philandering St. Croix is merely another disguise." Her tone became serious. "Which presents me with some very difficult problems. Why did you marry me and who are you really?"

Richard gave in. There was no point in trying to bluff it out. Her logic was impeccable and her intuition accurate. Much of his mission would be simplified with her knowing the truth. "We prefer to be called agents. Reconnaissance agents to be precise. Spy sounds so ugly."

Rose went to stand directly before him, inviting his embrace. "There, that wasn't so hard, was it?" she asked as if to a small boy.

Richard pulled her to him, enclosing her slim body with his arms. It felt so good to have no more lies between them. "I'm glad you know, my darling. I wanted to tell you, but the importance of the mission demanded that no one know. I needed you to act just as you have, as the unhappy and confused bride of a philandering cad, even though to do so tore at my heart. Can you understand, my love? Can you forgive me?"

"What is there to forgive? Do you think I would condemn you for loving and serving England? Your honor and duty are what make you what you are, Richard. I would not change that."

"But you said yourself you know not who I am. Frankly, sometimes, I'm not certain I know who I am."

"Perhaps. But there have been glimpses. The hero who saved Aunt Bernie and me. The man with the fine mind who can realize long-term results. The chess player. The man who loves puns. The lover whose caresses bring me such delights. Yes, there is much I can deduce from these hints."

"As for why I married you. Quite simply, I love you. To be honest, I had no intention of getting leg-shackled when I went to Copter's office that day, despite Sir Michael's urging. But when I saw my prospective bride was the beautiful, courageous woman from the coach, I could not refuse. I didn't realize it, but I was half in love with you even then.

"Sir Michael wanted you to marry me? He didn't even know me."

"Not you precisely. He thought the wedding trip would be an excellent cover for my mission."

"I see. And how do you feel about all this now?" Rose asked.

Richard had been prepared for that question. He scooped her up and carried her to the bed where he proceeded to show her just how he felt.

Rose snuggled against Richard's shoulder, basking in the warm glow left from their lovemaking. He tamped out his cigarillo and turned toward her.

"The question now, sweeting, is how do we get you out of Paris without raising eyebrows?"

Rose looked up into his face. "Why should I leave Paris?"

"Because, now that you know my real reason for being here, it is unsafe for you to remain."

"You will have to explain the logic of that. How am I in any greater danger than I was before? Are you afraid I might let something slip? I may not have as much practice at dissembling as you have, but I assure you, I can handle anything that might come as a result of your activities. Besides, I could actually be an asset to you. Do you realize how much is said at these soirees and teas I've been attending?

It wouldn't surprise me at all if some of the tidbits I overhear would nicely round out the information you are gathering."

Richard slipped his hand along her cheek and caressed its softness. "Rose, this is not a game. It is a very risky business. Do you know what the penalty for spying against Bonaparte is? An extremely slow, painful death."

"All the more reason for you to have someone else to back you up. I'm sure Hamstead is very good . . ."

"Gillis, John Gillis." Richard interrupted her to supply his friend's real name.

"Yes, er, Gillis is very good, but you must admit it would be helpful to have someone here, on the home front so to speak, while the two of you are out doing whatever you need to do."

She had a point, Richard realized. "Very well. But you are not to try to do anything to assist me other than explaining my whereabouts should the occasion arise. And, if I do not return from some rendezvous within the appointed time, you are to grab Tillie and make your way to the yacht as quickly as you can. I do not want to have the additional worry of your being trapped by Bonaparte's men."

"But, what about you? I could not leave France without you."

"Yes, you can and you will. I am perfectly capable of looking out for myself. Not having to worry about your safety will make it that much easier on me. Can you understand this?"

"I am not a fool, Richard. I would not create a situation that might distract you from your mission. I can understand how worrying about me could be detrimental to your survival instincts."

Pleased with her answer, Richard kissed her forehead and continued. "I promise you, my darling, when this assignment is over, I shall quit the service for good. The life of a spy . . ."

"Reconnaissance agent," Rose reminded him with a smile.

"Is not one for a married man. I will settle down to the quiet life on my estates where we will raise our children in bucolic contentment. There will be no more wild adventures for me. Just the adventure of loving you."

Rose pulled back from him and looked into his eyes. Though she said nothing, she knew that Richard could never be content living the quiet life of country aristocracy. But now was not the time to cross swords on that point.

"And," Richard was saying, "you can begin your new role this very evening. I'm afraid I won't be able to escort you to the Heath's dinner party."

"That should be no problem. I could probably get Pietro Giorello or Edward Lassiter to act as my escort."

At the mention of the Italian's name, the image of Rose throwing herself all over the man rose full-blown in Richard's mind. "Speaking of Giorello, what was that all about this afternoon? I wanted to kill the man and wring your neck."

"Oh, that," Rose said in a small voice, a babble of laughter belying her meek tone. "After I recognized you, I was afraid Pietro might as well. I realized there had to be some clandestine reason for your behavior, so I sought to distract him from noticing you."

"You certainly succeeded in distracting him and about twelve other men on the Promenade. I don't know whether to thank you or spank you. It isn't the sort of conduct one expects from the Viscountess St. Croix."

Rose laughed. "I hardly think that you are a wife beater, Richard." But she scuttled to the other side of the bed just in case.

"If we are to continue the charade, I must get

dressed. I have several appointments before the dinner party and I still have to contact Edward."

"Don't let that young fool take advantage, Rose." Richard warned, disgruntled at her escape.

"Richard, he's two years my senior, so I would hardly call him young. And he is always a perfect gentleman."

"Those are the ones you have to really watch out for."

The Heath's dinner party was a small affair comprised entirely from the English community. After the meal was served, the guests were expected to provide the entertainment with musical renditions or recitations. Rose gritted her teeth as one young man regaled them with his version of an Irish ballad. Unfortunately the man's voice did not have the range the song required and he squeaked on the high notes.

"This is perfectly dreadful," Edward Lassiter whispered to her after yet another sour note.

"The poor man should try learning an instrument instead," Rose acknowledged, trying to hide her amusement.

"With any luck, he will bust a stay in his corset and we shall all be saved from enduring this torture," Edward leaned closer to Rose.

She pulled back a bit, not wishing to invite any of the problems Richard had warned her against. "Now, Edward, we must be charitable. What is your contribution to be?"

"Me? Why, I had planned on reciting the "Begat" passage from the Bible. That should put everyone to sleep."

The young singer ended his rendition to polite applause and several not-so-polite comments from his contemporaries. Matilda Heath performed next, playing on the pianoforte with more technique than talent, but at least it was a respite from the sour notes of the previous performer.

"And what are you planning on regaling us with, Viscountess?" Edward Lassiter whispered directly in her ear.

Rose was becoming annoyed with his barely hidden attempts at seduction. "I think I shall play 'Greensleeves' and have done with it."

"An excellent choice. I know, I shall lead the ensemble in a group sing while you play."

"As you wish."

Robert leaned back in his chair, pretending to stretch and brushed Rose's shoulders with his fingertips. "I must say, Viscountess, you look exquisite tonight. What a pity St. Croix isn't here to feast his eyes on your beauty. Where is he, by the by?"

Rose turned indignant eyes on her companion. "Edward, you have been a good friend since we arrived in Paris, but I will brook no undue familiarity. If you touch me again, no matter how casually, I shall tramp on your foot with the heel of my Parisian pumps. As for St. Croix, I suspect he is probably at that gaming hell you and the others introduced him to. Oh, don't sputter. It makes you seem like a schoolboy."

Lassiter was indeed sputtering. Never had he expected such a forceful response from a well-bred English woman. She should have said "Phashaw" and tapped him with her fan. This open promise of physical violence took him quite unprepared. "I assure you, Viscountess St. Croix, I mean no disrespect. Indeed, it is just that St. Croix neglects you so. Surely you can pardon the unfortunate moth who cannot help but fly into the flame."

Rose, seeing his sincere contriteness, gave in. "Very well. But do not let it happen again." She turned back to the music. What is Richard doing tonight? she wondered. Is he in danger?

At that moment, Richard was back in the Bois de Boulogne, waiting to meet with the disgruntled captain one more time. They had changed the point of the rendezvous slightly so they were now deep in the trees by a lean-to. These small structures were no more than a few sticks with branches thrown over the top and had been used by the royal gamekeepers to store traps and other paraphernalia for the royal hunts. This one sagged to one side and most of the roof was missing.

"Gillie, go up near the road and keep a sharp watch. This spot is far too close to the highway for my comfort."

"Aye, sir. Are you sure about this man? Seems to me he picks much too open places for meetings. If he is a suspect, or a double agent, we are sure to get spotted."

"I know. That's one of the reasons I'm not letting him see any part of my anatomy. A man has been identified on a ring or the tassels on his boots. This whole thing just doesn't seem right. Yet, his information is proving accurate. I have been able to confirm it through my other contacts."

"You be careful, Major. If for no other reason than I don't want to have to explain what happened to you to your missus."

Richard gave a little laugh. "No worries there, Gillie. She's on to us."

"The devil you say. How?"

"Well, old friend, partly because of that gold tooth of yours. She recognized you as one of the men who rescued her on the Guildford Highway. Oh, don't feel badly, she saw through me, too. Thank heaven the French aren't so quick-witted."

Gillis grunted at that and turned to take up his position a few yards from the road.

Richard slipped into a thicket that grew at the base of a tall pine. The sharp twigs stabbed at him despite his thick cloak and he had to take special care not to receive any scratches that would be hard to explain later. Even so, one managed to evade his hands and lashed him in the cheek. "Devilish way to live," he muttered. "Here I am sitting on the hard ground, being pricked and prodded by stones and branches when I could be in a nice, comfortable inn room with Rose in my arms and a brandy in my hand. Stanton, you're a fool." His mumblings were cut off by Gillis's whistle. Someone was coming up the road.

Richard forced himself to remain motionless, even controlling his breathing so that the sound would not attract attention. He heard the trod of heavy boots coming through the brush. They stopped a few feet from his position.

"There can be no liberty under a dictator," a voice whispered. Richard recognized it as belonging to the captain.

"And that dictator is Napoleon," he replied. "What news do you have for me tonight?"

His contact stepped closer to the thicket. "I overheard a conversation between Minister Fouche and one of the admirals. The flotilla that Bonaparte has been building in Marseilles is sailing to join the fleet at Nantes."

"What route will they take and when will they arrive?"

"The admiral said something about sailing up the Garonne to Bordeaux." "As for when, I heard no date. Soon, I think. I . . ." he never got to finish what he was saying.

From the direction of the road, Richard heard the sound of horses and men's voices shouting. "Over there, by that tree!" They had spotted Gillis! Every fiber in his body longed to go and help his old friend, but he knew to do so could be fatal to them both.

Unfortunately his contact was not so coolheaded. He began to run.

"Look, another! Catch him. It seems our information was correct, after all, Gerrard."

Richard sank further in the thicket. To bolt would only insure his capture and the loss of all the information he had garnered. "Get away, Gillie. Get away," he silently prayed.

Two shots, one from a pistol, another from one of the new rifles that Bonaparte had equipped his soldiers with, rang out. There was a scream from somewhere to his left. His contact, Richard realized. More scuffling, the sounds of breaking branches and boots on dry leaves, a yelp of pain from near the road. Two pairs of legs passed his hiding spot. Richard could see the limp body of the captain between them. The branches of the thicket hid much, but he could see the grotesque visage that had once been a face.

"Where is the other one?" the voice that had given all the commands demanded.

"He is gone, *mon capitaine*." The speaker's voice was weak, as if he were in great pain.

"Jean, take Angier to the hospital. The rest of you, search the area. He may be hiding."

Sweat broke out on Richard's brow and ran in rivulets down his face. He could taste its salt on his lips and it stung his eyes. These he closed tightly, lest some stray moonbeam catch their whites and give away his position. All around him the sounds of the search continued. Richard remained immobile, breathing slowly into the front of his cloak to muffle even that small sound. At least Gillie had gotten away. Thoughts of what his own capture would mean invaded his attempts to remain calm. It wasn't that he was afraid of dying. That went with the job. He was far more afraid of living. No human could resist for long the tortures that Bonaparte's agents would use on him to extract what information he had. To calm these disturbing thoughts, Richard called to mind Rose's sweet face. He concentrated on building an image as he had last seen her, soft and warm and contented after their lovemaking.

The search circled back to his thicket. Richard clenched his fists and subdued his breathing even more. The cold ground chilled his legs and backside, causing painful cramps, but he daren't move. He strained his ears to pick up everything the soldiers were saying.

"There is no sign, sir. He has gotten away."

"No matter," the commander's voice replied. "We have killed the traitor and we have a good description of his accomplice. There must have been another, though. The one by the road was probably a lookout. No matter, we will track them all down eventually. Back to the barracks. There is no more we can do here this night. We will bring a tracker back at first light to pick up the trail." The boots spun and headed back toward the road.

Richard stayed in his cramped hiding place a full half hour before he crawled from its concealing depths. The welt on his face smarted and he was stiff with cold. It would be a long trek back to the horses, if they were even still there, and an even farther ride to the hotel. He'd have to take a circuitous route to ensure the French hadn't left someone behind to watch the area. His hand touched something sticky as he pulled himself up. It was the blood of his contact. Richard stared at the dark smear on his hand, turned black by the moonlight. Sometimes the price of freedom was dear indeed.

Rose tried to calm herself and focus on the fancy piece she was embroidering. She had returned from the Heath's party expecting to find Richard waiting, safe from his excursion. Instead, there had only been

Tillie. The maid helped her undress and ready for bed. Still, there was no Richard. Finally Rose had sent Tillie to bed and settled herself by the hearth to wait. Was this how it would be; her waiting anxiously for some scrap of news that her husband was alive? Despite his words, Rose felt she should have gone with him. Certainly two lookouts were better than one. She could keep an eye out for Bonaparte's men just as well as Gillis could. It would have been far better than this endless waiting.

A scratch on the door sent her flying to release the bolt. "Richard!" she exclaimed, the name dying in her throat as she recognized Gillis.

"Hamstead! How dare you return drunk. Come in here this minute!" Rose said for the benefit of two curious men in the hall. She drew the older man into the room.

"Mr. Gillis, where is Richard? Is he all right?" she demanded.

"He's not here, my lady?" Gillis was puzzled. "The meeting was over three hours ago. He should have been back by now."

Rose poured the man a hefty brandy and handed it to him. She indicated one of the chairs by the fire. "Sit down and tell me what happened."

Gillis did as she directed and took a hefty swig from the brandy. "Yes, thank you, my lady. Can't figure why the major's not back yet." Seeing the worry on Rose's face, he hastened to continue. "Not that there is anything to worry about, my lady. And I would be more comfortable if you would call me John or just Gillis."

Rose noted that he said "my lady" to her in the same way he called Richard, "Major." The observation gave her some pleasure as it meant that this colleague of Richard's accepted her in their tight circle. "Then, John, tell me what happened."

"There be nothing to tell, my lady. The contact

came; he and the major talked; and Bonie's troops stumbled on me. I got away. The major had plenty of warning. There's no need to fret. He's gotten out of far worse with nary a scratch on him."

"I'm afraid not this time, Gillie." Richard's voice came from the bedroom doorway. He lightly touched the welt on his cheek. "Still, it could have been far worse."

"Richard!" Rose exclaimed and ran to his arms. She hugged him to her, wanting to make certain he was real, there, and unharmed.

Richard drew her close, inhaling the sweet perfume of her hair. He nodded his approval when Gillis quietly slipped out.

"Let me see your face," Rose said, her momentary joy giving way to more practical matters. She placed her hands on either side of his jaw and examined the red weal there. "A cool compress should take care of that, if it doesn't bruise. It it does, well, I fear Viscount St. Croix will have to use powder and rouge to disguise it if he is planning on going out in public tomorrow."

"Alas, I must. For St. Croix to miss a race would be unthinkable. Some of the young officers are setting up a derby in St. Germain. They invited those English who are known to have deep pockets to provide the betting. No doubt, they see it as a way of having some fun and fleecing the English at the same time."

"You could have a toothache and wrap a cloth around your face," Rose suggested.

"Now then I really would look a quiz." Richard grimaced in the mirror. "Well, let's try the compress. Maybe that will turn the trick." He kicked off his boots and went to stretch out on the bed. It gave him great pleasure to have Rose fussing over him.

Rose, aware that Richard's eyes were on her, enjoyed the little wifely chore of pressing the cool cloth to Richard's cheek. She bent down and kissed him lightly on the nose. "I knew I should have gone with you. Another lookout would have given you more warning. How did you escape the troops?"

So Richard told her the events of the night. When he had finished, Rose kissed him again, this time full on the mouth. Richard pulled her down on his lap and cradled her in his arms.

"It will all be over soon, my love. Just one more meeting in the Palais Royal and it'll be done. In fact, you can start making plans for a departure. Of course, we must give some plausible excuse."

Rose put her hands on her hips and moved them seductively. "How about the viscount is tired of his wife's wanton ways and has decided to drag her back to England and shut her up on his estate?"

"Wanton, zounds, everyone thinks you are the sweetest of innocents. I am the cad in this piece, I'll thank you to remember."

"Well, I don't see why I can't be just as wicked as you are," Rose objected.

One corner of Richard's mouth went up in a piratical sneer. "It would behoove you greatly to remember what happens to wicked little ladies. No, I think the best thing would be for me to lose a huge sum at Madame LaRoche's tomorrow night. Enough to make everyone believe we are on the rocks. That would explain our sudden departure. Especially if we slip out without paying our bill."

"Richard, the staff here has been very cooperative. I would hate to leave without paying them what is their due."

"Very well. Since it's still early in the month, we'll have Gillis pay the current bill tomorrow morning, before I drop ten thousand or so."

"Ten thousand! This spy business is certainly expensive."

Richard laughed. "Don't fret your pretty head

about it. Madame LaRoche is one of our people. I won't have to really pay the money. Don't worry, your inheritance is secure."

"I wasn't worried about that, Richard," Rose protested, fearing he misunderstood.

"I know. But, as for your part, you might reemphasize your concern over my wastrel ways. Have you any engagements tomorrow?"

"An *al fresco* at Madame Tallien's and a literary discussion at Lady Whitworth's. Then the Heaths have invited us to attend the *Comédie Français* with them in the evening. I think the literary group is an attempt on the ambassador's part to make things appear normal. There is tremendous strain between Lord Whitworth and Bonaparte. Lady Whitworth confided in me tonight that she fears Bonaparte's rudeness can only be regarded as the preludes to a declaration of war."

"Interesting." Richard looked at her for a moment. "Any other little tidbits you have picked up lately? Oddly enough, some of the information you have garnered over the teacups has confirmed what my contacts have been giving me."

"Well," Rose thought, delighted she might be able to give him some additional information. "Madame Junot was disconsolate that her husband would have to leave Paris, but now she is quite happy because someone else is taking up the post. A General Merian, or something like that. The romance between La Belle Pauline and the Borghese seems to be coming to fruition, despite Pauline's lapses when she's around any handsome male. Oh, yes, Bonaparte has insisted that the ladies stop exposing themselves in public. Josephine and the other ladies of court are all having gowns made of opaque fabrics."

Remembering Rose in the sheer dress she wore to the opera, Richard grinned, "I'm glad to hear that."

"Oh, one more thing. Madame Junot seemed inordinantly curious about Scotland and Ireland. She seemed to think that, because I am English, I know all about those countries."

"That is curious. But Madame Junot is, after all, only nineteen and a bit of a feather-head anyway. She was probably repeating something she heard. Most likely it means nothing, but I'll make a note of it. There have been some rumors that Bonaparte is trying to get a foothold in either of those countries."

"But that would be terrible! Scotland is right on our borders and under our protection. Ireland, I grant you, is forever a problem, but Bonaparte's presence would be intolerable."

"That is for others to worry about, Rose. We must deal with our own mission."

Rose rather liked the way he included her in the task ahead. She snuggled closer. "As you say, my love. But we have pretty well hashed that out, haven't we? There is still one thing I need you to make clear for me."

Richard looked down at her. "And what is that, sweeting?"

"Just what does happen to wicked little ladies?"

Chapter Fourteen

THE MORNING OF April 6, 1803, Paris was washed clean by a gentle shower that scrubbed the city's streets and walks and gave new life to the budding trees and flowers. Rose threw open the casement of the large window in their bedroom and took in deep breaths of the sweet, rain-filled air. Behind her, Tillie was readying her toilette.

Richard had slipped out an hour earlier. The red mark on his cheek was all but gone and a touch of Rose's face powder had hidden what remained. The race was to take place at mid-morning and he had an hour's ride ahead of him.

Rose thought back to his leave-taking. He had bent over her and kissed her lightly, promising to be back in time to escort her to the theater that evening.

A loud knocking at the suite's front door sent Tillie scurrying into the next room. Rose heard her arguing with someone.

"You can't come in here. Her ladyship is not receiving. Stop pushing, you big oaf!"

"Madame la Vicomtesse will see us, now. This is not a social call." A deep, masculine voice, his English heavily accented, delcared. "Bring her to us."

At the first sound of the trouble, Rose threw on a

heavy wrapper and tied it securely around her waist. How dare they treat poor Tillie so! She entered the front room just as a soldier was giving Tillie a little shove.

"There is no need, Tillie." She turned withering eyes on the officer in charge of the two other soldiers. "By what right do you invade my morning tranquillity, Captain?" she asked in French.

Relieved that he wouldn't have to struggle with the difficult foreign tongue, the officer's attitude softened. "We wish to speak with Monsieur le Vicomte, madame. I have an order from the proconsul authorizing my presence."

"I see." Rose moved over to one of the chairs by the hearth and sat down, for all the world like a queen holding court. "Well, Captain, I'm afraid you have just missed him. Perhaps there is something I could help you with?"

"Monsieur le Vicomte has a manservant, no? A man in his forties with a gold tooth?"

"Yes. That sounds like my husband's valet, Hamstead," Rose acknowledged slowly.

"We wish to speak with him." The captain motioned for the two soldiers to remain by the door and crossed over to where Rose was sitting.

"But I just told you, my husband is not here."

"Not your husband, the manservant." The officer was getting impatient.

"But why should you want to talk with Hamstead?" Rose tried to stall to give herself time to think.

"Because, madame, he was seen participating in a rendezvous with a known spy. There is one other man, but no one saw him. We wish to be assured that this Hamstead is indeed the man who was spotted. It is not difficult to speculate that the other man was the viscount."

"St. Croix!" Rose pretended surprise. "It is obvious

you are not at all acquainted with the viscount if your thoughts are running along those channels. Unless there was a game of chance involved, St. Croix would have been nowhere near this place. Where was this meeting held?"

"In the forest of the Bois."

"There, you see, that proves it. St. Croix absolutely loathes anything remotely rustic. And as for Hamstead, I grant there seems to be some superficial similarities between him and your quarry, but it ends there. The poor man barely speaks three words of French. I doubt he could find his way much further than the East Gate without getting lost. No, Captain, I'm afraid you've followed the wrong scent. No doubt, since he is English, some disgruntled citizen chose to point him out simply from patriotic zealousness. But I can see you will not be satisfied until you have seen Hamstead. Tillie, ring for the man."

Tillie picked up her cue like a veteran actress. "But Mr. Hamstead isn't here, my lady. He went with his lordship this morning."

Rose spread her hands in apology. "There you have it, Captain. You are welcome to search the premises if you wish." She waved him toward the bedroom door. "You might begin in there. Perhaps he is hiding under the bedstead."

The officer stiffened. "That will not be necessary at this time, Madame la Vicomtesse. However, you should bear in mind that, at the moment, you are considered only a bystander in this incident. Your failure to cooperate with us could change that status very quickly."

"Why, Captain, I am nothing more than a helpless Englishwoman alone in a strange land. What threat could I pose to anyone?"

"Madame, we French have long appreciated the abilities of beautiful women. Madame Guillotine can testify to that." With that threat, he signaled the two soldiers to follow him and left.

"Give them about an hour and then check to see if they have really gone. If they have, find Hamstead and bring him to me. We must make plans."

"Coo, my lady, is it true, what that Frenchie was saying? About Mr. Hamstead being a spy?"

"I couldn't say, Tillie." Rose decided the little maid didn't need to know any more than necessary. "But until we find out, don't let anyone see you bring him here."

Rose returned to the bedroom to finish dressing. She had just gotten her morning gown on when there was yet another intrusion into her rooms.

"My lady, it's the innkeeper. I can't make heads or tails of what he's saying," Tillie informed her.

Rose went to speak to the hotel manager. "What may I do for you, monsieur?"

"Oh, Madame la Vicomtesse, I am so sorry to be the bearer of such sad news. You must not think badly of us, madame. It is the times, nothing more. Never have I had such gracious guests as yourself and the viscount. You have honored my hotel with your presence." The man continued to ramble on.

"Yes, yes, monsieur, but what is the problem." Rose tried to keep the fear out of her voice. Had something happened to Richard? Had they captured Hamstead?

"The proconsul has declared war on your country, madame. First Consul Bonaparte has issued an order that any English found within the walls of Paris after seven o'clock this evening will be imprisoned." The proprietor wrung his hands in his anxiety.

"Where did you get this information?"

"From my cousin. He works at the Tuileries. He knew that I had English guests and did not want me to lose any money."

"It has not been generally known then?" Rose was thinking rapidly. Richard had insisted that she leave at the first sign of trouble, but she could not abandon him to certain imprisonment and likely execution!

"The criers will announce it at noon. Since you have been such gracious guests and paid your bills so promptly, I wished to inform you as soon as possible."

Rose sent over to the little desk and opened the drawer that held a small pouch for miscellaneous expenses. She withdrew it and held it in her hand. "You have been most kind, monsieur. I wonder if I can prevail upon your generosity one more time. We shall need a traveling coach in about two hours. One capable of making the run to Dieppe as quickly as possible."

"I shall see to it, Madame la Vicomtesse." The proprietor accepted the pouch. "In two hours," he promised as he bowed out.

"Oh, my lady, what are we going to do?" Worry creased Tillie's normally clear forehead.

"You and Hamstead are going to take the coach, with as many of our things as you can manage, to Dieppe. The viscount and I will join you later. Now, fetch Hamstead to me. We must plan."

By the time Gillis arrived, Rose had pretty well formulated what her actions would be. They were frightfully daring, something that no typical lady of quality would attempt, but Rose was willing to risk everything if it meant a chance to get Richard out of France safely.

"John, where is Richard's meeting tonight? I know it's in the Palais Royal, but that place is such a warren, I would never find him."

Gillis listened as Rose outlined her plan. After making a few suggestions, he reluctantly agreed to it. "Very well, my lady. But the Palais Royal isn't any place for a lady to be wandering around alone."

"Then I won't go there as a woman. Do you and Richard think you are the only ones who can change their appearance with a little makeup and costume?" Rose turned to Tillie. "Now, let's get busy. Tillie, I need one of your dresses that the staff here has seen several times. That bonnet of yours, too. The one with the deep brim that shadows your face."

While the maid scurried to fulfill her wishes, Rose turned back to Gillis. "I do hope you like vermilion, John," she said as she pulled a full-cut monk's cape complete with hood from her wardrobe.

"Bit bright, isn't it, my lady?" Gillis took the garment gingerly.

"I want everyone on the street to see the Viscountess St. Croix and her maid entering a traveling coach and leaving Paris. Now, try it on, Viscountess."

"The major isn't going to like this." Gillis grumbled as he wrapped the red folds around him.

"You leave Richard to me, John. You just get Tillie safely to the yacht and have it stand by off of the spit of land we saw before we entered Dieppe harbor. If we haven't signaled you by midnight four days hence, sail back to England. We can't afford for both of you to be captured. I take it Richard shared the information he has gathered with you, in case something should happen to him."

Gillis nodded. "That's standard procedure, my lady. I've got everything except what he picks up tonight."

Tillie returned with the dress and bonnet. "Why do you want my clothes, my lady?"

"Because," Rose patiently explained, "the staff here is used to seeing you go up and down the back stairs. By wearing your clothes, I hope they will take me for you and pay me no attention."

"Coo, my lady, that's right clever," Tillie exclaimed.

"I thought so," Rose acknowledged the praise with a smile. "Then I plan to make my way to a market and buy some secondhand boys' clothes."

Gillis could tell that Rose was getting caught up in the adventure of the situation and thought it behooved him to put in a word of caution.

"My lady, we do strange things in this business, but if we want to survive, we are cautious, very cautious. Generally, 'tis safer in a crowd than alone because you are less noticeable. Being a boy might be a good idea, but you have to really be a boy. Boys don't take genteel little steps and hold their pinkies up when they drink tea. And, begging your pardon, my lady, boys don't have full bosoms and narrow waists."

Tillie gasped at Gillis's bluntness, but both ignored her.

"I know, John. When I was in school, I performed in several productions, mostly Shakespeare. I played the male parts as frequently as I did the female. Now, I'll slip down the back stairs as soon as I've changed into Tillie's clothes. The coach should be brought around in about another hour. That way, if anyone does see me, they'll assume Tillie has been on some errand and returned. Tillie, try to pack up as much as you can, but don't let anyone see you for at least half an hour." Rose went over to Richard's trunk and lifted the lid. She removed a small wooden chest, which she unlocked with a key Richard had given her. Inside were several franc and English pound notes and three pouches of coins. Rose took the franc notes and handed one of the pouches to Gillis. "You'll need this to pay the tolls and post. It might be best if you hide the rest with my jewel chest. With the mad exodus that is bound to take place, brigands are certain to be on the road."

With that, Rose retired behind the screen to change. When she came out, she had on Tillie's blue